SURPRISE!

SHARON HEALY-YANG

Surprise!

By Sharon Healy-Yang
Published by Sharon R. Yang
www.sharonhealyyang.com

Copyright © 2025 Sharon Healy-Yang
All rights reserved.

Softcover ISBN: 979-8-9920155-1-5

Digital ISBN: 979-8-9920155-2-2

Cover Design: Karasel Cover Art

First Edition 2025

Printed in The United States of America.
www.sharonhealyyang.com

Also by Sharon Healy-Yang

Jessica Minton Mystery Series

Bait and Switch
Letter from a Dead Man
Always Play the Dark Horse
Shadows of a Dark Past

October, 1939, Massachusetts.

Smart-talking mystery writer Vicki Westlake accepts a dare from two old-time friends: spend a night in the type of house that would give H.P. Lovecraft the willies. Even the dissuasion of a third friend can't stop her from taking up the challenge. Once left alone, Vicki finds herself *not* alone for long. A car accident on the deserted roads sends concert pianist Janos Husaruch to join her, a man with a brooding past and an unexpected connection to Vicki. That's not Vicki's only surprise, for she and Husaruch discover something upstairs much more terrifying than a spooky dare. Before the storm-tormented night is through, Vicki and Janos, as well as her three friends who unexpectedly arrive, will find themselves stranded in a house of death, death ever hungry for more victims.

Chapter One

Saturday, October 14, 1939 confronted Vicki Westlake from the top of the paper she'd purchased at Boston's North Station. One day earlier might have been more appropriate. Well, what lay ahead of her in Lowell didn't require a prophetic date to disturb her more than this jouncy train ride. Or worse, recent headlines about further economic wobbling, passenger and merchant ships mined or shot to oblivion, and politicians fretting that this war of '39 could plague the world for another three years. For only one uncomfortable flash did the dark-haired young woman in her even darker trilby hat and trench coat admit that some nether part of her mind had been dreading this day.

She jerked her head to the rain-splattered train window. Dreary swamps and ponds, dangerously swollen, blurred together as the train picked up speed after the last stop. Wilmington, was it? What should have been a forty-minute ride had been elongated another twenty when the train had periodically slowed to a plod, the engineer probably afraid of flooding. At least she wouldn't have to swim in. After one more stop (another fifteen minutes or so?), she'd be in Lowell. Lucky her.

Testily, Vicki debated which was sillier: her inability to resist picking up a tossed gauntlet or her anxiety over the situation into which this failing had entangled her.

Vicki Westlake caught her reflection staring back at her, superimposed over the soft slur of sodden marshes and ever-darkening skies. Shoulder-length, wavy chestnut-brown hair; long oval face; fair skin over high cheek bones; arched brows and slightly almond-shaped green eyes, characteristically elfin, now hard. Friends often described her as an impish Dresden shepherdess, but the face staring back from the window was insurmountably grim.

1

That's when she burst into a delighted little chuckle. She hadn't been summoned to an interrogation by the Gestapo. She was merely going to settle once and for all that her pal David Morrow could not intimidate her. He'd been trying to get the better of her since they had been kids together, inflicting mud and snowballs on undignified portions of each other's anatomy. They'd still known each other when he was at Harvard Law School and she had been at Wellesley, before too much investing on the margin had caused her father to lose all their money, and she'd had to drop out to help support the family and later fund her younger brother Ben's plans to become an architect.

Back in the neighborhood and then in Catholic school, she and Sunny, Tim, and David had really come together, though the boys had been a little bit older. Yes, David of the devilish blue eyes, the wavy jet hair, and the insouciance that had attracted many a woman. Vicki had decided that David was a good, fun friend but no sure thing as a romantic prospect. It was a darned good thing, too, that she'd never let herself become one of those women. After tonight he'd remember one thing—never to needle her. He'd remember he'd had to eat his words. David Morrow might have been a honey of an investment lawyer, but he'd be singing a different tune after tonight. He'd see beyond a shadow of a doubt that Vicki Westlake was a far cry from the weak sister he thought.

Again the delightedly insidious little chuckle. This time, Vicki instinctively sobered under the skeptical eye of a middle-aged, grey fedored commuter a seat or two across the aisle. A slightly arched eyebrow and a charmingly superior play of her lips prompted him to drop his eyes and pull the collar of his overcoat up around his jowls. Seeing him back down, Vicki still glanced about, uncertain how much attention her chuckle had drawn. Two older women in tired wool coats and worn, sensible shoes read assiduously directly across from her. Snoring seemed to emanate from behind her. It hit Vicki rather sadly that her fellow passengers were, unfortunately, too preoccupied with their own troubles—would their children be dying in foreign wars, would they themselves even have jobs tomorrow? Why should any of them waste time wondering about her eccentricities? Did that make tonight's challenge between her and David a bit petty?

Vicki turned emphatically to her newspaper. Had she actually let David set her up? Did she really want to do this? Tonight? Was it...well, of course it was safe. She had nothing to worry about. Where was the entertainment section, anyway? Oh, good. Yes, here. The young woman paused. Amidst movie, play, and symphony advertisements was an interview with Janos Husaruch. *Aha!* Even a picture: long face and sharp strong jaw, aquiline nose, but the face was saved from aristocratic frigidity by eyes that (even in black and white) snapped dark and humorous and cheeks curving as roundly as Claudette Colbert's into a smile. The young woman laughed lightly, inwardly, at herself. Here she was, twenty-nine-years old, and she had a crush. Well, it wasn't as if she were going to run into him over a head of lettuce at the grocer's.

Vicki scanned rapidly past the standard biographical information: born to a working class family in Lawrence, Massachusetts, thirty-nine years ago; studied at the Curtis Institute, then Europe; the death of his wife and his return to Europe to forget the pain—here's where she slowed, straightening in her seat with interest as she hit the new information: last March helping a Czech family escape the Nazis' less-than-one-week silent conquest of Czechoslovakia. Vicki flinched, reading Husaruch's first-hand description of the relentless, inexorable German takeover without firing a shot. There was something about funding music scholarships, then benefit concerts for refugees, leading to his well-spoken insistence that he had seen too much of the Axis consumption of Europe whole not to view neutrality as self-destructive, never mind unethical.

What an intelligent, decent man, Vicki reflected leaning back against leather upholstery, the line of her mouth softening with quiet respect.

Abruptly, Vicki shook her head to break her reverie and closed the paper. Why did she have to be just as silly over someone she didn't even know as some teenagers were over, well, Clark Gable? David and Tim loved to kid her on this score. Anyway, she liked to see that there were people who could still care even in this dark time.

The paper was folded and put away as the train slowed. In the requisite inarticulate diction of his profession, the conductor announced what many trips on the Boston/Maine line had taught Vicki to decipher as "Billerica." A few people got up, moved down the aisle, and disappeared from her adventure. "Adventure?" So *that* was what she was calling it now?

3

Why did David have to read Ambrose Bierce, anyway? What was the name of the short story that had gotten the whole Megillah going? Oh yes, "Suitable Surroundings," a disturbing little literary number that touched on the power of atmosphere and imagination to overwhelm a reader's reason with terror. The four friends made a point to get together twice a year and this "adventure" had to be the fruit of their latest luncheon. But the one to propose the plan hadn't actually been David; it had been Tim. Tim West once again trying to impress David—or were they all guilty of that, Vicki grudgingly pondered. He might be charming about it, but David did have a way of making you want to impress him. Maybe not Sunny, though.

The train's lurch forward briefly interrupted Vicki's line of thought. Her glance fell on the newspaper. She, Sunny, and Helen (a friend from the publishing company where she'd once worked) would be going to Husaruch's Boston benefit at Symphony Hall. He was doing "The Mephisto Waltz," among other pieces. She'd first heard his performance of the Liszt several years ago, thanks to an aunt who'd kept a wonderful classical collection; the Husaruch version was from his early European recordings. Vicki couldn't suppress the deep, from-the-soul sigh, re-experiencing the fury, the power, then the restrained mystery and devilishness of the music Janos Husaruch had created. Could a wax disc pour out such feeling, such life? And wasn't she being a grade-A dope, reliving her immersion in the satanic Mephisto's power right before Tim took her to The House?

Think about Sunny. Sunny would be joining her and Helen at the concert next week. Sunny was such a sweet friend to have. People might enjoy Vicki's tart humor, might take the time to see there was generosity and loyalty beneath; but Sunny, Sunny was the one everybody loved from first sight to long past parting. Sunny was the grandest person anyone could know. Even a proper businesswoman's tailored gray suit and black gloves could not counteract her smile-rounded cheeks; sweet-laughing hazel eyes; and ear-length, soft, curly wheat-brown hair. Sunny insisted that her nickname was the result of her determination not to plow through life under the appellation of Harriet, but her friends thought differently.

What a pity Sunny had gone and married Bob Addams. None of them could have expected her to do it. They'd all tried to talk her out of it, even

4

David, especially Tim. Tim loved her. He always had, even though he'd never say it. Maybe she could help him now, knowing what Sunny had been saying recently about Bob. But should she? Shouldn't she let Tim and Sunny work things out for themselves, or did Tim just need that little push? It was a difficult play to call.

It had to be hell for Tim, running a real estate office with Sunny—the office that had enabled him to come up with the house for tonight. So now he could impress David with his proposal to put Mr. Morrow's creepy little challenge of her into action. Always, ever since Vicki could remember, Tim had driven himself to impress David—and David had egged him on. So now was Tim going to help David get to her, using that old, dark house on this storm-blasted evening? Or, here Vicki calmed on reflection, maybe Tim was looking for her to help him take David down a peg. That wouldn't bother her one bit.

Vicki sighed. What a group of friends. Things got really complicated for childhood pals when they grew up. Ah, Tim was only human—and lonely. He and Sunny should have married; then they'd all be happy. Well, those two anyway. She'd still be unattached and David would still be chasing skirts. Not that she was fixated on David. It wasn't as if she'd held a torch from him since that summer years ago. Heck, she'd even been jilted once since then. Hmm, maybe her judgment of men wasn't any better than Sunny's after all. The right one just never seemed to show up. Maybe God was saving Janos Husaruch for her. That thought brought another ironic smile to her features.

The train lurched in the newly increasing wind.

I was kidding, Vicki mentally chided with a heavenward glance. Looking down again, Vicki noticed her other reading material: two battered paperbacks, editions of *Dracula* and of a Guy de Maupassant collection including "The Horla." Her pause was miniscule before she stacked one book on top of the other and pressed both, face down, on her newspaper.

Sunny had violently objected to their plan. Sunny rarely lost her temper, but when she did, well, the contrast with her characteristic "sunniness" never failed to rattle Vicki, even after all these years. Only settling on a house in Belvedere had calmed Sunny, or at least left her resigned. She was much less foolhardy than any of them.

The train was slowing, and Vicki only now truly recognized they had entered the city. Sitting up straight, Vicki unconsciously clasped her dark-gloved hands, and glanced over at the old women again. She really started this time, but now with pleasure.

Delight curved her features into a smile. One of the women had pulled out and was reading a mystery novel, her, Vicki Westlake's, novel. And she looked intense, absorbed! Vicki resisted the impulse to intrude, but she did cross her legs with languid satisfaction, her cat-green eyes and upturned lips doing the same service as a self-assured purr.

Writing was something she could do like no one else she knew. She certainly didn't pretend to be any Virginia Woolf, but she could create and keep people in suspense, delight her readers. And now she even made enough money to live comfortably. But the most important part was the creativity. That was something that David, with all his wealthy clients and Harvard Club lunches, couldn't buy or charm his way into.

And she knew *he* knew this truth, too. That was why he had thrown down his playful challenge for her to prove herself, to prove her imagination wasn't ultimately a weakness by living out a variation on the Ambrose Bierce story: spend a dark, stormy evening in an ominous, isolated old house without becoming victim of "better" writers and of her own imagination. Vicki knew that even if this evening scared the living daylights out of her, even if she was being every inch as foolhardy as Sunny had said, she would not let David Morrow chalk her up as just one more foolish gal, too irrational to cope with the real world. No match for the pragmatic "realities" of which David Morrow, lawyer, was master. To be honest, too, it would be nice to help Tim pull the rug out from under the man who had always one-upped him. And the best part of the whole deal was that David would have to undergo a similar test after hers!

Still, something did continue to eat at her. When Tim had called to make arrangements for tonight, Vicki had pressed him on how he and David intended to know for certain how she'd fared during the night. She could have just pictured Tim grinning as he'd mysteriously replied, "We've figured that out; don't worry. But telling you would only ruin the surprise."

The train jerked into the station and Vicki sheepishly smiled at the melodramatic complement to her equally melodramatic interior monologue. It wasn't as if David were ready to join all four of the Axis powers as the nemesis of humane civilization. He had taken time and energy to help her invest her earnings wisely so that she could live in a nice apartment in town. He'd even been a supportive friend when her engagement had gone south. He could just be a royal pain sometimes in the way he looked at women. You didn't have to be Eleanor Roosevelt to see that. He needed to be taught a lesson to straighten him out. And she was the gal to do it.

Vicki gathered her purse, overnight case, and books. A swift glance at her watch told her they had run about twenty minutes late. At 5:40, it still wasn't quite dark, just ominously overcast. However, the wind had graciously made up for the lack of lightning by tormenting the rain with vicious swirls dashed into the ground. When Tim picked a dark and stormy night, he wasn't kidding.

As other passengers began to shuffle along the aisle, Vicki turned up her black trench coat's collar and pulled down the brim of her trilby against the rain. Standing up, now that the commuter traffic in the aisle had dissipated, she decided that at least being late would mean she wouldn't have to wait for Tim. Probably. Tim could be a trifle scattered at times. He was smart to have teamed himself up with Sunny's practicality.

Pausing from stepping down from and out of the shelter of the train, Vicki studied the gray cold and cutting wind and rain, nervously worrying her worn leather watchband. You couldn't have come up with a night worse than this, short of moving to Transylvania. Head bowed against the night, one hand clutching down her hat, the other tucking books and newspaper close to her and away from the elements, Vicki made a dash to the station entrance. She impatiently had to wait to enter, behind the last of the commuters. Glancing at the mackintoshed men who rushed handcarts of mail into an alley adjacent to her and the express office, Vicki sourly pondered why the number of people crowded before you at the entrance always increased in proportion to the foulness of the weather.

And now, once inside the spacious waiting room, there was no Tim. *I'm late and still there's no Tim.* A quick scan of the room revealed a long ticket counter just to her right; a flock of people heading for the doors opposite her that led to a waiting fleet of Yellow Cabs; intermittently filled wooden benches; and, to her left, double doors marking the front entrance. Vicki walked slowly across the wooden floor, debating whether to sit down or wait for Tim outside, under the cobblestone arch that extended across the crescent drive to Middlesex Street. What had Tim told her to do? He hadn't been all that clear over the phone. He'd been in a rush and just said he'd meet her here. With Sunny in and out on some special project, poor Tim had been pretty harried. Vicki forced herself to stop worrying her watchband before she broke it.

Maybe it would be better to wait outside so Tim wouldn't have to worry about parking. He could just drive in off Middlesex Street, pause to pick her up, then zoom around the crescent back onto Middlesex. She probably wouldn't have to wait too long. The arch ought to be enough protection, although it was getting raw with the wind and rain.

Tim West must have heard her thoughts. Vicki had no sooner stepped outside than his dark blue, 1934 Chevrolet sedan nosed its way into the drive and around the curve to her. Tim pulled up and Vicki wasted no time getting in, eager to get tonight's plot rolling.

"Good. I *did* tell you to wait outside. I couldn't remember," Tim distractedly greeted her, a handsome man with wavy, wheat-colored hair under his fedora, kind brown eyes, and a slightly crooked nose that made him look slightly and charmingly off-kilter. He apologized, sheepish but grinning, "Sorry I'm late."

"Just as well. We were late, too, getting in. I don't even remember where I was supposed to meet you."

"You're late?" Tim glanced at his watch and started. "Darn. I had no idea. I just rushed here after I wrapped up. Didn't even look at the time. I still have some paperwork to do after I drop you off. What a day!"

"You *are* excited about tonight, too?" Vicki queried hopefully.

"That's the good excitement. The not-so-hot excitement is that Sunny took off early. She got a call and said she had to leave for Boston in a hurry. I'm her partner and she won't even give me the low down on why she has to dash off to Boston on business."

"Cheer up, Tim," kidded Vicki, putting her hand on his arm. "It'll be my turn to be exasperated tonight. And you certainly picked a perfect evening."

Tim cracked a real smile at that, glanced back to make sure it was safe to pull out, and responded, "It may be even more perfect than you realize. I've been hearing reports about thunderstorms."

"Thunderstorms?" Vicki felt a little foolish at the trace of excitement in her voice. What? Was she Colin Clive anticipating making a monster in one of those *Frankenstein* movies? Well, even if it was a little odd, she did enjoy a good thunderstorm, though her motives were somewhat less satanically scientific than the good Doctor's.

"Isn't it a little late in the season for thunderstorms, Tim?"

"How many years have you lived in New England?" her companion queried good naturedly as they pulled out onto Middlesex Street.

Vicki laughed, lifting her hat off and shaking out her hair, agreeing, "That's true. I should know better than to question *any* scrap of weather around here. Anyway, I do enjoy a good storm."

"Then you should be delighted tonight. They always seem to follow the river, and you'll be almost sitting on it."

"I hope I'm not washed away. Wait a minute. I don't know Lowell that well, but I didn't think Belvedere was on the river."

"It's not, but you're not going to Belvedere tonight. At the last minute, I changed my mind. I decided that you might find the thought of neighbors too comforting, so I'm putting you in a nice old place in Tyngsborough — not too far past the bridge, but far enough out that you'll be perfectly isolated. David and I used to go hunting in the woods around there."

"Thanks. Will the closets be rattling with skeletons?" Vicki quipped.

"That's up to you and your imagination," Tim responded evenly as he bore to the right where the road branched at a red brick school.

They passed a rain-greened park to their right and Vicki commented, "I certainly hope you will pick an equally creepy setting for David."

"I'm trying to buy real estate in Transylvania now, or I might just invite him to my wine cellar for a little Amontillado; I'm double checking the crypts," Tim assured her, his eyes twinkling.

"You're an evil man, Timothy West."

"It's the real secret of my charm."

Vicki smiled, then changed the subject slightly, "So, Tim, what did Sunny say about the newly selected site? Does she still disapprove of our little experiment in terror?"

"Who knows? She hasn't been around long enough to talk to. She's been awfully distant lately, Vicki. I'm a little worried."

"Do you think it has to do with Bob?" Vicki asked carefully.

"Again, Vicki, who knows? She won't say. I try to talk to her, but she shuts me down. The poor kid is so wrapped up in making things right for everyone else, she won't talk when something's eating her. She won't admit something's wrong. Doesn't she realize we're her friends? That's what we're here for—to help her when she needs us. I wish she'd let me help. Sometimes she can be awfully stubborn...cold."

Tim had spoken levelly, but Vicki could tell he was hurt—hurt for Sunny and hurt that she had shut him out. Vicki could find nothing pithy, effective, original to say. She hesitated to say anything to Tim of what Sunny had recently told her about her marriage. She wasn't sure if Sunny had been telling her a confidence or one of those pseudo-secrets that people sometimes revealed in hopes that you might pass on what they were too timid or uncertain to say themselves. An uncomfortable silence hung between her and Tim.

"There's a nice place for David," Tim broke the unsettled silence, nodding his head to the left at a cemetery they approached. "I mean for his evening out."

"Oh, I thought you had other kinds of plans. I didn't think that you were *that* irritated with him."

As they drove past, Vicki turned her head to study the old headstones rising above them on a grassy swath of ground almost atop a stone fence. She remarked, "What an interesting cemetery. It looks so antique."

"I think it's the oldest one in the city," Tim pointed out.

"Hmm. I'd like to go back and look it over sometime. Would it be allowed?"

"I don't know, Vicki. I guess you could always pretend you were looking for your Great-Aunt Hepzibah or something." Tim smiled, adding, "David doesn't know what he's got himself in for, making this kind of a bet with a gal who likes to explore cemeteries."

"I just like the peacefulness and the, I guess, antiquity. You don't have to make me sound so ghoulish. I *don't* want to dig up the bodies," Vicki laughed.

Tim smiled before explaining, "Anyway, now we'll be driving through an old-money section of town, so you can indulge another one of your other passions—old houses."

"Hmmm, maybe I am a little Gothic at that."

Vicki and Tim both enjoyed critiquing the various edifices they passed. She expounded on the beauties of Victorian houses, and he pointed out each preference of hers was a lot of territory for one petite girl in a trilby to occupy.

"After supporting my family in that tiny apartment these past years, Texas wouldn't be too much territory for me, if I could have some privacy."

"Well then, you should love where I'm placing you tonight," Tim quipped, devoting his main attention to the mergence of the street they traveled with another on their left.

"Spacious dungeons, elegant cobwebs, secret passageways?" Vicki inquired.

"I don't want to ruin your surprise," Tim returned, briefly endowing her with his smile.

"Nazis smile like that," Vicki dryly observed.

"We aren't at war, yet, Vicki. Let's not get political."

"Mmmm."

"What book did you bring?" Tim changed the subject to neutral grounds.

"De Maupassant's 'The Horla' and *Dracula*. Ever read them?"

"I saw the movie of the latter. They even had a nurse in the theater for it; publicity, I guess. I don't know de Maupassant. I guess I've heard the name somewhere. Does he write much in the way of horror?"

"Not usually. Characteristically, he sticks to the ironic, but this story, urgh!" She shivered on the last word. "It's a delightful little tale of a man stalked by an invisible, intangible, *indestructible* being that's sucking his will and very life force from him. I must tell you, Tim, I read it first when I was twelve and literally couldn't sleep with the lights out for two weeks afterwards."

"You *are* taking this seriously!" her friend beamed.

"Of course. However, we'll have to make sure David is as honorable as I am about his selections."

"I agree. No allowing *Little Women* because he's always been afraid of Louisa May Alcott."

"You said it!" Vicki laughed.

Finally, the two grew quiet as they moved further from the main part of the city. The houses became sparser. They passed a small sports field

11

on the left and a handy hot-dog stand near it. Tim commented that the latter had the best shakes and hot dogs he'd ever experienced. He admitted that quite a few nights, when work had been tiring or drawn out, he and Sunny had gone there, thrashing out problems with each step and rewarding themselves, sometimes as late as midnight, with hot dogs and shakes.

"Some time you'll have to treat me, too, under more felicitous circumstances," Vicki suggested.

"Tonight, you'll have to make do with some coffee that I brought for you in a thermos," Tim consoled her.

"Did you do that? That was a nice thought."

"I'm a nice guy."

"Hmm. Will you pack some coffee for David, too?"

"Definitely. But his will be cold."

"Poor David. Now wipe that cat-that-ate-the-canary look off your face."

Tim further explained, "Of course, there's no telephone, gas, or electricity, but I did arrange for the water to be turned on, so if you want to make some tea in the fireplace, or, need running water for, shall we say, other 'essentials,' you would have all the comforts of home."

"Albeit a somewhat haunted home?"

"You read my mind, Vicki."

They lapsed into a smiling silence. The houses along the roadside grew even fewer. Trees and breaks of rain-enriched grass predominated. At some point, Vicki became aware that Tim had turned on the radio. An Artie Shaw tune soared and swayed into the car, and she caught her finger bouncing along in rhythm. It was almost as if there were no darker, "bigger picture" to worry about in the world. She watched the river when the trees permitted; it was choppy and high and an unfriendly gray. *So, Thoreau canoed up this? Not on a night like tonight, brother.*

"The Merrimack isn't as bad as it was last year?" she queried, a touch nervous at the memory of the big hurricane and flood.

"Nothing's *that* bad. Why? Afraid of being swept away? Maybe you don't need the books after all."

"Don't worry, Dracula. I can swim."

"You're going to be on high ground. The basement would be a mess if you weren't, around here."

"Swampy?'

"You're very near the river."

"I imagine on a nice day this must be a lovely place. Great for walking, not on the road, mind you. Good for fishing. In fact, the main industry along the road seems to be bait stores."

"I see there are a couple of diners."

"I bet they serve mainly fish."

"No, they have human clientele."

Vicki didn't respond, verbally; she just gave Tim a long, hard look.

"The rain does it to me, Vicki."

"Mmm hmm."

The roadway to their right was clearer. Railroad tracks hugged the river. Vicki could see a large steel bridge spanning the Merrimac up ahead, around the river's curve.

"We're going across?"

"Yes."

"Not to New Hampshire?"

"No, we'll still be in Massachusetts. But the road gets tricky. I have been up here to check on the house before, so I know my way. There are several little, well actually, narrow but long roads off this route. They all connect the houses on them to this main. route But there's a lot of property in between, so if you don't count carefully, you'll easily miss the right road and end up at a hostile householder's. There's always a reason people like to be so isolated. Anyway, Vicki, these roads are murder to find at night, so it's a good thing we're getting here before it's too dark."

They hadn't gone very far beyond the Merrimack when Tim signaled a left at one of the lonely side roads and turned off the main way. In better weather, the fairly wide dirt road might have been quaint, albeit a tad bumpy. Now the soupy going made travel an obstacle course as Tim played dodgems with puddles the size of Lake Michigan.

"Nice scenery," Vicki deadpanned.

"Now you know why the house is still on the market."

Vicki smiled, turning her attention back to the trees, or rather woods, that lined the road. Normally, one might have called this a tree-shaded drive, but in the cloud-shrouded twilight and relentless rain the trees seemed almost oppressive, crowding a road that seemed to invade their territory.

They drove on for some time, prompting Vicki to query, "We do have a destination, don't we?"

"The former owner liked privacy."

"I'll say. Antarctica was too crowded for him?"

Tim grinned, adding, "Almost there."

The road twisted slightly and gradually elevated into a hill. A slight clearing appeared so that Vicki could see a stone wall framing a light-painted, two-story affair. They pulled up at the front door.

"Home at last?" Vicki queried. Before Tim could answer, a low rumble did the honors for him.

"Hmm, an omen?" Vicki pondered dubiously, positioning her trilby back on her head.

"I promised you a thunderstorm," Tim gallantly replied.

The rumbling grew louder.

They got out of the car, Tim taking Vicki's case. Yet even as Vicki turned up her collar to protect her hair against the wet, she still didn't dash in to avoid the rain. She stepped around the car and back from the house to take stock. With tenants it would have seemed unprepossessing, at worst austere, like its isolationist owners. Somehow, uninhabited, the sharp lines, the gray paint, the dark windows, the Indian shutters sealed tight inside the windows, and the tall and scraggly shrubbery encircling the house from the rear and partway to the front windows all made the place seem almost displeased at her presence. How dare she intrude on its peace, its privacy! It had become used to being unencumbered by people.

"The reading light's much better inside," called Tim from the small porch, where he had unlocked the front door.

"What are you complaining about?" Vicki lightly chided as she rushed up to join her friend. "At least you're out of the rain."

Vicki entered the house and glanced around the good-sized foyer as Tim disappeared through a doorway to the right, beyond the pegs on the wall for hanging coats and hats. She dropped her overnight case under the pegs, on the floor. Those floors were hardwood, expensive hardwood. On the left wall, double-doors closed off what was probably a study. Before her, to the left, an oak staircase ascended to a landing, abruptly angling off into the next flight leading to the second floor. There was a window on the landing bordered with panes of stained glass. No sunlight gave the glass luster tonight. The wallpaper was a rich burgundy with black spiral designs. Gloomy, but dignified.

Vicki perused the rest of the foyer. To the right of the stairway, directly across from her, was a single door. A closet? Egress to the dining room or kitchen? Then she stopped, abruptly recognizing an anomaly about this house for sale.

"It's still furnished?" Vicki queried to the room on her right where Tim was busying himself at the fireplace, his trench coat and hat stowed on a chair.

"You can't take it with you," Tim returned without turning from his task.

"I guess not," Vicki agreed, entering the living room, pulling off her gloves, and stuffing them in her pocket.. "I guess I just never pictured so much remaining behind."

"No relatives to claim it except the distant niece who had to sell us the proverbial 'lock, stock, and barrel' so she'd have some money to live on."

Vicki looked around the room, commenting, "But everything seems clean. No mustiness. No dust."

She approached the dark red drapes of the curtained picture window to her left, listening as Tim explained, "Sunny sees to that. We never know when a buyer or renter will come along."

Vicki had opened the indoor Indian shutter and, after a quick peek through the curtains, turned back to Tim to smile, "Aren't you grand, building me a fire!"

Tim turned his upper body from where he knelt, setting up kindling, and grinned, "I can't have you expiring from damp and cold."

"I see," observed Vicki, crossing to Tim and the hearth on the opposite side of the room. "The only fatal shivers I'm allowed have to be from terror."

"Precisely," agreed Tim. "Oh, and I put several quilts in your bedroom upstairs, third door on the left, in case you decide the couch is too stiff for sleeping on."

"Won't the sheets or the mattress be musty?"

"Sunny sees to everything."

"Hmm, what's she running here, a motel on the side? You know that might be the reason you've never rented or sold this house."

"Go hang up your coat and hat on a peg, next to the front door. Let me get this 'cheery blaze' going in here. You're going to need all the cheer you can get tonight." Tim chuckled with mock malevolence.

"Heh, heh, heh," Vicki teased back, grinning and giving her friend a salute of acquiescence before returning to the foyer.

Stashing her hat and coat in the foyer, her books held tight, Vicki hoped that the kelly-green jersey she wore would be warm enough. The material was warm, but the sleeves were short. She smoothed down her skirt of cream and kelly chevron stripes and adjusted her wide green belt as if girding herself for battle by looking her best. Now she proceeded back into the room where Tim was fanning the kindling to build up the fire.

"What? No roaring hearth yet?" Vicki kidded.

Tim feigned a growl as he worked on the fire, then tossed over his shoulder, "You could help."

"No thank you. You're doing fine without me. Anyway, Tim, you know I don't like fire," Vicki replied, sitting down on the couch before the hearth. The promised thermos sat atop a long, low mahogany coffee table separating her from the fireplace. *Ah, the coffee! And a large flashlight!*

Tim paused in his uncomfortable crouch, again turning to Vicki in the gloom and said, "I hope you can light matches now. You'll only have candles here."

"I can light the candles from the fireplace, smartie."

She leaned back on the couch, an arm comfortably extending across its back and glinted her sardonic cat's eyes at her friend.

Tim grinned again and nodded toward the thermos, "I see you spotted the coffee. Plus, there's a quilt over there," a nod to her left and a nearby chair angled toward the hearth. "As I told you, there's no electricity or telephone. So I left you that flashlight next to the coffee. If something happens to it, there are more in a cupboard in the kitchen. You have mugs, tea bags, and a kettle in there if you need more than this coffee. Between the flash and the firelight, you should be able to read well enough. Oh yes, there are candles in the kitchen cabinet and in the library across the hall."

Vicki teased, "For someone trying to scare me to death, you're making me awfully comfortable."

Thunder lowered, much closer now.

"That's so you won't be too comfortable," Tim smiled devilishly.

He checked the fire again and muttered, "Oh good," seeing the flame steadily licking away at the two containing logs. Tim seemed to forget about Vicki, concentrating on determining the right moment, then reaching across to his right and adding a larger log for the insistent flames to feast on. Her companion's preoccupation left Vicki with the uncomfortable leisure to reflect again about him and the importance of what Sunny had said recently about her rocky marriage.

She heard Tim telling her not to let the flames bank down, to stir the embers with the poker to keep the fire going, to add kindling when necessary, not to smother the flames with a log that was damp or too big. Vicki wasn't completely listening, though. Her once more worrying that watchband was the only indication of an inner debate over whether to tell Tim what was really on her mind.

"Vicki?"

"Yes?"

"You listening?"

"Mmm, hmm. Stir, add, don't smother, no dampness."

Tim smiled, as if deciding his little plan was working. The hearth light was beginning actually to give Tim, of all people, a decidedly Satanic glow. Vicki almost expected him to rub his hands delightedly. Tim, however, did no such thing. He just turned back to the fire to give the flames an unnecessary, proprietary little poke.

"Tim? What will you do if Bob doesn't come back from Havana?"

Vicki wished her friend would say something. He didn't. He just crouched there, back to her. Had he heard? Should she repeat the question? In the gloom, she couldn't be sure if her question had made her friend's shoulders tense.

"What makes you think Bob won't come back?"

Vicki almost started when Tim broke the silence. He still wasn't facing her. The fire received a sharp poke.

Vicki leaned forward, her hands clasping her knees.

"It's Sunny. Tim, she was, well, almost relieved about Bob's going away. She kept dropping these funny hints, kind of hard to put your finger on, but I don't think she expects him to be coming back—and she didn't seem at all disappointed at the prospect. Has she, has she said anything to you?"

Tim barely glanced over his shoulder at her. The fire crackled, but Vicki didn't feel cozy or comfortable now. Well, Tim did need some prodding. He was too nice a guy to be stuck in limbo, and Vicki had had the feeling Sunny might want some sort of go-between. Still, being a go-between was not a role with which Vicki felt at all comfortable. But wasn't her friends' happiness more important than her own comfort?

Finally, Tim stood up, glanced at Vicki, then moved over to the far side of the hearth, getting the screen and placing it in front of the fire.

"Keep this in place. You don't want any sparks setting fire to this carpet."

"You're going to drop the entire subject, aren't you?" Vicki didn't accuse, but her sympathetic tone did have an edge of challenge.

Tim turned sharply, "What do you want, Vicki? It's all rather up to Sunny, isn't it? It's her life."

It might have been the yellow glow behind him, but the firelight aura in the dark room gave Tim an unnervingly furious cast. Vicki slowly sank back into the couch.

Seeing her trepidation and regret, Tim shook his head, "I'm sorry, Vicki, It's just all hopeless, useless. Believe me, I know. I just hope I haven't looked like a fourteen-karat dope to everyone."

Vicki reassured him, "Not at all, Tim. I'm just concerned. I'm amazed at how well you can carry on a professional relationship with her, the way you feel. No one could criticize you."

"Except for David."

That tone was bitter, bitter enough to make Vicki flinch. Tim's regret was immediate. He shook his head, looked away, apologized, "I'm sorry Vicki. I can't blame you—can't even blame David for my failures."

"I'm not talking about failure, Tim," Vicki disagreed, concerned. She moved around the coffee table to stand before her friend in the shadows beyond the fire. Vicki shivered a little, but continued, "Don't mind David. You know him. Someone left the safety latch off his sarcasm. He doesn't mean half of what he says. And he always apologizes.

"As much as we fight like cats and dogs, he's even done me good, Tim. David made me laugh again after I was jilted. He helped me find financial security and peace of mind when I was so afraid of putting my savings anywhere but under a mattress. He even introduced me to my editor..."

"Yeah, he helped me fit in, make connections, at college. He helped me with his connections after I finished. I guess we all owe David Morrow."

Vicki frowned. Tim's tone hinted a twinge of jealousy at a friend whose success he could never quite match. This was not what she'd had in mind.

"Tim, forget David. That's not what I've been trying to get through to you. This is about *your* future. You calling the shots for yourself. If you have a chance with Sunny, grab it. Stop waiting for her to fall for you. Do something about it. If her marriage to Bob is really over, then make your pitch for a life together. And if that doesn't work, well, at least you tried and you can be free to move on to someone else."

Tim blinked at Vicki's compassionate but determined words: "Forget, about Sunny?"

"Not forget exactly, but stop carrying the torch. Look, I'm really sorry if I've been out of line, Tim. It's just that you're a good guy, and I hate to see you hurting yourself. You deserve to be happy. Don't let deceptive dreams keep you from, well, living."

Tim watched her, puzzled, then finally said, "What brings all this on anyway, Vicki?"

She shrugged and shook her head of chestnut hair. "A lot of things. Sunny was talking, and I've been thinking. This world's so crazy and mixed up. Who knows if we'll even be here five years from now? It just seems, sometimes, maybe you have to take a chance, because you never know if you'll get a second one."

"Vicki," Tim smiled, not completely at ease, "you're talking as if you have war nerves, and we're not even at war." He hesitated at her worried expression, then touched her arm and chided lightly, "Goosebumps? Go sit near the fire. Have some coffee, wrap up in a comforter, pick up a book, and scare yourself to death."

Vicki smiled back, but as she moved back to the couch she could see that Tim still seemed a little troubled. Feeling guilty, as she sat down, Vicki began, "You're still upset by what I said. I'm really sorry, Tim. I guess David's not the only one who doesn't know when to keep quiet."

Tim's features tensed; he hesitated, seeming to need to tell her something. Finally, he exhaled and just cautioned, "Be sure to extinguish the fire before you go to bed. Don't leave it unattended."

"Sure," Vicki agreed, unhappy that she'd upset her friend, yet uncertain how to set things right.

Again Tim hesitated before adding, "There are some extra quilts up in the bedroom, remember? You're sure you'll be okay?"

"Of course." Vicki tried to reestablish their initial lightness to reassure him. "I'm tougher than you and David put together. Go ahead, just try to scare me!"

"Really?"

"You sound relieved," Vicki teased, relieved, herself, at having shifted Tim's mood. "It would take more than you two clowns to make me crack. Do your damnedest. I'm already looking forward to putting you two in your places. I'm ready for you."

Tim brightened, pronouncing, "Spoken like George Raft in a prison movie." Smiling, he added, "Okay then. I'll be here in the morning to take you home—what's left of you."

Vicki dismissed his threat with an imperious flip of her hand, then asked pragmatically, "Shall I call you?"

"Not unless you have an extraordinarily loud voice. Remember, there's no phone here."

"You got me there."

"So, you're all set? Any questions?"

"Well, one, again. Really, how are you and David going to know if these 'suitable surroundings' and a heavy dose of the Gothic make me give in to my fears tonight? I'm dying to—oops, bad word choice—I'd *love* to know. Will you two be hiding in one of the closets?"

Tim slowly shook his head, eyes glinting humor, and answered, "That would be telling."

Vicki narrowed her eyes at her friend, but then shrugged and said, "Okay, okay. I give up. I'm all set. You just drive carefully in the rain, my friendly tormentor."

Smiling like a kid, Tim added, "Don't forget the extra quilts in the bedroom upstairs. Remember, it's the third room on the left. It gets pretty chilly here."

Before Vicki could wise crack, "How thoughtful of someone trying to scare me to death," Tim West was gone.

Vicki was alone in the shadowy living room. To an apartment dweller this space was immense, even overcrowded as it was by furniture—just a bit too dignified to be considered 'twenties kitsch. *But doilies everywhere!* Vicki navigated back to the picture window and pulled back the curtains fully. It was still pretty gloomy, despite the opened curtains and crackling fire. Of course the dark wallpaper and the heavy furniture didn't lighten things up much—neither did the cloud-blanketed sky or the forests beyond the stone wall or the shrubs surrounding the house. And Tim was right; away from the fire the damp shivered through her small frame.

Surveying the room, Vicki decided Tim had made a shrewd selection in choosing this house. It wasn't so much creepy as inhospitable to intrusion. Nothing heavy handed, just unsettling. Who would have guessed Tim could be so diabolically subtle? Sometimes you just didn't know about people.

Smiling to herself, Vicki returned to the warmth of the fire, letting her attention roam over the objects stationed through all eternity on the white mantel. Funny that a clock, bronze candlesticks, and a framed photograph of a young man and woman in trendy attire of ten or so years ago should outlive the house's occupants. Furniture, what an odd memorial, but perhaps a telling one. Vicki had never really considered what her apartment said to others about her. *How archeological! It was like spending an evening in a Babittesque pyramid.* She wondered if this was how the slaves buried alive with their Egyptian lords in the pyramids felt. A tiny, but undeniable shiver, snaked up her spine. *Touché again, Timothy West.*

Vicki's glance turned again to the couple in the photograph. They seemed young. He was a little older. Her bob had been quite stylish back then. She couldn't have been responsible for all this old-fashioned furnishing, could she? Could they both be dead now? If they had been the owners, then they'd have to be, according to what Tim had said earlier. But they wouldn't have been that old. Or were they even the owners, after all? Just friends or family? Vicki smiled. *Tim could have even planted the photo. Well, that attempt to be scary fell flat. The couple didn't exactly look like Mr. and Mrs. Dracula.*

The thunder was growling now, much nearer. Ah, time to get down to work. Vicki settled herself on the couch and flipped though her book to find "The Horla." The fire was warm enough, when you were right in front of it, even if the house itself wasn't. Thunder snarled again, even closer. Maybe she would have some of that coffee.

Chapter Two

Even as he entered the outer office of his business, Tim was surprised, that his and Sunny's secretary, June, had packed up and gone home. Even the *Photoplay* that graced her desk for lunch-hour reading was gone. But she was supposed to stay late to help him clear up some accounts.

"June?" he queried, puzzled, before noticing that although the door to Sunny's office was closed and her lights out, his office was open and illuminated. *What the heck?*

Maybe it was the mindset of tonight's mission, but Tim automatically tensed at the sound of movement in his office. He took a hesitant step forward, but that was all he dared manage.

"I thought Vicki was the one trafficking in ghosts," David Morrow commented wryly at Tim's reaction as he emerged from the private office, a tall, well-proportioned man in his early thirties with wavy black hair, a long jaw, and devil-may-care blue eyes.

Tim's eyes closed briefly in relief before he answered, not inhospitably, "What the hell are you doing here?"

"Aren't old friends welcome?"

"Where's June?" Tim queried, removing his wet trench coat.

"I sent her home. You work that girl too hard. Yourself, too. Come back into the office. Let's dip into your private stock. Looks like you could use a shot."

Tim wasn't sure how, but he found David had graciously ushered him into his own office and had set both of them up with shots of Johnny Walker from the hideaway bar. Rain splattered against the windows overlooking Merrimack Street. David's driving gloves were cast carelessly on Tim's desk.

"Fine. Now that you've welcomed me to my own office—what're you doing here?" Tim questioned as he hung his coat and hat on the coat stand also holding David's.

David shrugged from the chair which he'd commandeered and answered, "I had a meeting with a client here in town. Could I have picked a more miserable day for a drive? I thought I'd drop by when I finished up. Unfortunately, no one was around but the hapless June. Where were you and Sunny anyway? Doesn't anyone work around here except the secretary?"

"Sunny had a call. She went to take care of something in Boston; she left without giving me the details," Tim absently explained. Then brightened, continuing, "I, on the other hand, have just finished executing a masterpiece of staging."

"Oh?" David's curiosity was slyly piqued.

Having the upper hand with golden boy David Morrow, Tim enjoyed himself immensely. He proceeded to play David's curiosity like a marlin, "I set Vicki up in a house across the river."

David had to think a minute before smiling knowingly, "The evening of terror?"

"Precisely."

"We lawyers are sharp. Miss nothing."

Tim grinned, delighted to know something that David didn't.

"What?" David questioned, with that sardonic smile of his. "What are you leaving out?"

"Not much. I set Vicki up perfectly. That's all."

"Eerie house? Stormy night? Clever."

Tim continued to grin.

David regarded his friend with amused, intrigued skepticism: "And?"

"And," Tim continued, leaning back, enjoying the upper hand for once, "I provided Vicki with everything she needs: a good fire, a thermos full of coffee, a flashlight for reading, and—a nice turned down bed."

"Thoughtful. Now what are you leaving out?" pressed David, all charm. "You're not entirely on the up and up, are you old chum?"

Tim was still enjoying himself too much to give everything away just yet. He shrugged, savored his drink, and then solicitously pointed out,

"You haven't started your drink, David. Good stock. You don't know what you're missing."

"I know I'm missing something," David decided, enjoying the challenge.

Tim pretended to give his companion a questioning look before replying with mock recognition, "Oh, oh, you mean about Vicki? Let's just say I've made things interesting for her."

David deepened the devilishness of his smile and posited, "I take it you've prepared a little surprise of some sort for our friend?"

"You take it correctly. However, I doubt you've figured out how I'm planning to surprise her."

Was David a touch annoyed at not having the upper hand for once? He didn't look quite comfortable, even glancing distractedly at the dark windows as thunder growled outside. Still, David was too good a lawyer to wear his heart on his sleeve. He was all urbanity as he lit his cigarette and commented with a nod to the right, "Connecting door to Sunny's office? You devil, Timothy, my boy. I didn't think you had it in you. Mixing business and pleasure? Does the desk turn into a couch?"

"What?"

"Looks like a cozy set up to me. And you're right; this is nice stock. I bet Sunny gets a little kick out of it."

"Wait. We're not talking about Sunny. We're talking about Vicki," Tim tried to counter, more than a bit irritated by David's salacious raillery at Sunny's expense.

"Vicki doesn't 'work' in an adjoining office," David quipped knowingly, taking a leisurely drag on his cigarette.

"But she is going to find a pseudo-corpse when she turns in tonight," Tim cut in, wresting the conversation away from David's false innuendos about his relationship with Sunny.

"'Pseudo-corpse'?" David queried, his tone knowing as if he'd doped out Tim's plans already.

Tim sank back in his chair, realizing he'd been tricked into playing his hand before he wanted to. Of course David had struck at him through his weak spot, Sunny. He was damn sure he was going to enlist Vicki to think up an appropriate trick when David's turn came around.

"Let me guess. You hired someone to play dead."

"Mmm," Tim admitted, perturbed at having his cat sprung from the bag by David.

David nodded appreciatively, turning on his million-dollar smile for: "Good thinking, old friend. That ought to hit her nicely after an evening of reading horror stories by firelight in an uninhabited house in this storm. Stumbling into a dark bedroom with no electricity and only a flashlight for illumination—it shouldn't be hard to buffalo her into thinking she'd actually seen a dead body."

Tim relaxed. David's praise had almost erased his disappointment at his friend's tricking him into spilling the beans before he'd intended. Maybe even easing a little of that twinge of guilt over pulling a fast one on Vicki? *Well, she had challenged them to do their worst.* He finally added with a reflective smile, "And we'll both have the pleasure of checking up on the results later this evening."

David regarded his friend carefully before questioning, "We're going over there?"

"Certainly. We can't leave Vicki all alone in this storm. She ought to be quite ecstatic to see us, later this evening, after she's encountered my 'surprise.' In the meantime, could you do with a lobster?"

"Depends on what I'm supposed to do with it."

"Eat it. I'm ravenous, David. Being diabolic works up an appetite," Tim kidded as he put aside his glass and stood up. "But first, I want to make sure the connecting door is locked and get the keys if I have to. I don't leave anything unlocked here if nobody's around"

David got up, stubbed out his cigarette in a convenient ash tray, and pronounced, "Fine, but let's shake a leg. There are lobsters with our names on them waiting for us at—where are we going?"

"The Lobster Cot."

"Let's go."

* * * * * *

The slash of eerie blue light underscored the night-shattering thunder! A startled Vicki fumbled her book as if it were a trout flopping out of her grasping hands and onto the floor. Instead of retrieving *Dracula*, Vicki sank back into the couch as the thunder's glass-rattling reverberations through the house gradually subsided. *That bolt must have been darned close!* Of course, another bolt struck almost as near, illuminating the room with a peculiarly bluish light—but only briefly. If there had been electricity in the house, it certainly wouldn't be working now.

Vicki finally bent to pick up her book, carefully avoiding any corner-of-the-eye glances into the shadow-haunted crannies of the room. Between the storm, the firelight, and the inhospitality of the house, this room was definitely on the sinister side. Vicki's skin crawled with the same distinct discomfort of childhood nights when all bedroom shadows seemed to portray a gamut of ghoulies.

Needless to say, this was one storm that she didn't enjoy standing by the window to watch. In the view of the stone wall and the woods beyond, there was just something that smacked a little too much like God-forsaken Lovecraftian rural backwaters. The scraggly, thorny shrubbery clawing the edges of the window would seem way too grasping. Looking through the window would bring exactly the sort of sights only witnessed by those trembling alone. *Grrr, another fine mess.*

Vicki glanced down at the book on the couch, then abruptly up at the creaking ceiling. Of course, there was a stiff enough gale to make boards in this old house groan and complain. Her old pal had done his work well in selecting this place. Yup, tonight she felt tremendously less scornful of the people she'd called knuckleheads for being panicked by last year's Halloween present from Orson Welles over the radio.

Rising restlessly, automatically glancing around, Vicki was even a little surprised to find nothing fanged lurking in the shadows. She rubbed her arms, contemplating: go get her coat from the dark corridor beyond the firelight? No, it would probably still be too damp to be any good to her. So she stayed put because she just didn't want a damp coat. That was it.

Tim had said there were more quilts on the bed prepared for her upstairs. The dickens she was going up those stairs!

Glumly, Vicki sat back down. Even with the fire, it sure was damp. *Better damp than scared to death.* She inwardly squirmed at that admission. It was like ceding the game to David. *Damn.* Vicki sourly eyed the flashlight for a few moments before clamping her hand resignedly onto it. Why did she have to be so darned determined not to be beaten? It wasn't as if she were John L. Lewis going against G. M. for the United Mine Workers. Crossing towards the open double doors leading to the corridor, Vicki muttered to herself about self-respect not being all it's cracked up to be—but not too loudly. The flashlight created disturbingly misshapen shadows of the furniture. *Swell.* Vicki almost had to shove herself into the open, exposed foyer. *Hmm*, what lay behind the double doors across from her? Well, tonight her curiosity was somewhat less than incendiary.

This is stupid! It's not as if there really are things like vampires and Horlas. That you know of. Vicki glanced down the hallway at the door leading to what she suspected was the kitchen. Maybe Mr. and Mrs. Whoever-Had-Lived-Here-Before had left behind some garlic. Well, she had better put out that fire in the hearth before she turned in.

Ascending the stairs was no less disconcerting. *Why did that small landing angle about so sharply that you couldn't see what lurked (bad word choice) on the next flight of steps?* Vicki cautiously reached the landing, approached the turn, and nearly dropped the flashlight as lightning flared and snarled much too close.

She sank back against the wall with an unsuccessfully reassuring hand on her chest. Why couldn't she quite bring herself to brighten the stairway? Why wouldn't she directly look at the stairway ahead? *Because you're chicken, kid.* Thunder rumbled an affirmation.

Well, she certainly couldn't stand here all evening. Only horses slept on their feet. Besides, she would not for one minute let Tim and David say, "I told you so." Vicki's progress onward and up the stairs was determined, if not entirely confident.

The second floor was about what she'd expected, and that expectation was not calming. Facing Vicki was a large window which, thanks to lightning, provided added illumination to her flashlight. The floor sported a carpet running down its center, the windows possessed curtains, the walls were wallpapered with colors impossible to determine in the distorting storm light. Of course, she couldn't just go up the stairs and pop directly into her room. No, Tim had assigned her to the third room on the left. Vicki just knew that this room had to be at the end of the corridor. So thoughtful of her chum to provide her with a lovely little walk of terror.

Bravely, or, perhaps more accurately, stubbornly, Vicki proceeded, instinctively glancing behind her. *No one.* Just the wall on the other side of the house. Her attention returned to the corridor ahead. The *long* corridor. Lightning flickered through the window at the front of the house, the corridor's far end. *Why did this hall have to extend to infinity? Thanks a bunch, Timothy West.*

Moving cautiously through the semi-darkness, Vicki tried hard not to conjecture what lay behind the closed doors to her left. She'd had a nightmare once about a strange dark house and doors tempting her to open them. When she'd finally given in, there had been candlelight and an evilly smiling face, the face of a friend. Then there had come a knife flash. Vicki shuddered, not quite kidding herself out of anxiety by muttering, "What would Freud say?"

She shuddered again. Somehow the spoken word seemed an affront to the house's self-imposed isolation. She really did *not* belong here.

Vicki faced the door to "her room." Unpleasantly, she found herself considering the possibility that Tim might have found someone to lurk (there was that word again) inside to leap out at her when she opened the door. Fine. After she landed and stopped screaming, she'd flatten the creep with this heavy-duty flashlight. It wasn't hers anyway.

Vicki was surprised to realize that people really do take deep breaths before committing momentous acts—well almost before. Quirking the corner of her mouth with dissatisfaction, she poised her flashlight defensively and opened the door.

Nothing. Well, nothing outright threatening. Between her searching flashlight and the lightning, Vicki could pick out a bed in the center of the room, nicely turned down, perpendicular to the right wall. A nightstand with an electricity-dead lamp resided on the near side of the bed. There was a cold fireplace opposite the bed and a scatter rug on the floor between the two. The quilts Tim had promised were folded and stacked high and cozily on the bed. The rest of the room, as best Vicki could perceive, contained various furnishings one might expect to find in an older woman's bedroom/sitting room. There was a small bay window and window seat against the far wall, beyond the bed.

Despite the darkness and dampness, this room *could* have been comfortable—perhaps *would* have been if Vicki hadn't the distinct feeling its occupant might return any moment and rage at her for invading this private domain. Considering that the last occupant was dead, that impression was more than a little disconcerting.

Vicki closed the door abruptly behind her. To keep out that late occupant? To no longer feel like a general with her rear guard exposed? *Hmm, now that was a somewhat risqué picture. At least the room didn't seem at all musty.* Tim had done nicely by her in that respect at least.

So now she'd have to make herself comfy, Vicki decided as she fumbled with her watch while still trying to hold the flashlight. Finally having had enough with her fidgets, the band split, leaving the watch itself to tumble from her hands and bounce under the bed. A bed with a spread that almost reached the floor. Definitely, she couldn't wait to peer under a bed in an old, dark house. Now that she thought about it, she'd also had dreams about strange hands and other sorts of limbs snaking up to her from under a bed.

Resignedly, Vicki got down on her knees, pulled up the bedspread, and peered under the bed with the aid of her flashlight. No monsters, but the bottoms of a pair of men's shoes at first prompted her to conclude that separate bedrooms obviously hadn't prevented the owner of this room from enjoying herself—and then her smart-aleck attitude went poof as she quickly recognized that the position of those shoes and the bulk beyond it indicated that these shoes were occupied.

Vicki thought she'd scream—or at least drop the flashlight. Logic stepped in to head off both impulses. Tim hadn't failed in any other touches—why should he slip up here? It must be a dummy or maybe even a real person either playing possum to scare her or waiting to jump out when she least expected it. Well, then, she'd fix the little red wagon of this possible conspirator.

Vicki sharply pinched the leg that was too fleshy to be fake—and too clammy to be alive.

She screamed and dropped the flashlight.

* * * * * *

Janos Husaruch gave up. Swearing in Yiddish under his breath, he stripped off his driving gloves and shoved them into his coat pocket. His car inextricably caught in the roadside mire after slamming against a tree, he hesitated to step out into the driving rain. Like most sensible people, he had no particular fondness for being soaked to the skin. Looking skyward at the lightning raking across the surrounding treetops, Husaruch bleakly comforted himself that being fried by lightning would dry him off nicely. But he didn't get out of the car just yet.

At least his head didn't still ache. He'd suffered a bit of a thumping in the accident when his vehicle had done a 180-degree skid and slammed into the forest at the edge of this miserable excuse for a road. For a few minutes, he couldn't quite remember where he was and why he was out in the middle of a storm. He was pretty sure it had only been a few minutes. Then it had come back to him that he needed to be somewhere right away. That's right! He was supposed to get back home to Lawrence. No, Boston. He'd been to Lawrence for Shabbat dinner with his mother and siblings. No, again. That was last night. Today he'd been to lunch with Ric and Shana. They'd wanted to see the "souvenir" from Europe. He could feel it stiff against him inside his inner suit-coat pocket. But it had gotten dark so fast. His family would be worried about him traveling on a night like this, especially after what he'd been through earlier this year. It still came back in flashes, giving him the shakes.

Well, he wouldn't be getting the car out of this jam by himself. Come to think of it, driving down the road toward Route 110, he'd passed a house up on a hill, beyond a stone wall. Had its lights been on? Was there a car? He couldn't remember. Who'd have noticed trying to drive through this downpour? But since he didn't know this road very well and that was the closest house, the only house, he could remember seeing within walking distance, it looked like his best, maybe his only bet.

Grabbing his hat off the seat beside him, Husaruch pulled it on and turned up the collar of his black trench coat against the rain to venture grimly into the storm, hoping it wasn't his imagination that his head was actually less achy now.

Trudging down the dark, tree-lined road ahead, he assured himself that his destination couldn't be that much further. *Maybe less than half a mile. Maybe further. Think about something else.* Think about lunch with his friends, which his mother had tried to talk him out of earlier today. Janos replayed the tense conversation he'd had with her concerning his return to Boston this evening during a storm. He might have been well over thirty-years old, been married and widowed, achieved tremendous respect as a musician, lived in Europe off and on for over a decade, and escaped back here only a jump or two ahead of the Germans—but his mother still didn't want her son to go out in the rain. *What could you do with mothers?* Of course *Mrs. Husaruch's* automobile wasn't stuck right now; *she* didn't have to slog her way through a nasty storm to probably an empty building. *Where was that house anyway?*

By the time Janos Husaruch reached the stone wall, he was dismayed to see no lights coming through the house's windows. The house looked dead. Well, he'd be damned if he turned around now without at least checking to see if anyone was home. If he could just telephone his friends to come and get him. Still, it was a disquietingly dark house. *What if everyone were asleep?* Then someone would just have to wake up long enough to let him use the phone. Was he really asking that much? Even in the face of hostile home owners, being inside and out of this storm would be a damned sight better than getting soaked in this re-enactment of Noah's shining hour.

Husaruch dashed onto the small porch, at last out of the rain. Maybe he could even get some nice, warm tea—or some even nicer warming cognac? Or at least call Ric and Shana so they could give him a nice warm *anything*.

He raised his hand to knock, but before his fist landed the door flew open. There , holding a flashlight, stood the most horrified looking female he had ever seen in this country. At least she wasn't shining the light in his eyes.

"I came at a bad time?" he ventured.

Her mouth opened and closed, her free hand clamped on his arm. Janos Husaruch looked down at that hand, then back at her face.

"Are you all right, miss?"

She stared at him, her eyes darting annoyance only briefly before some sort of terror returned and drove her to back into the shadows of the house.

This is not good, Janos concluded. *I should get the hell out of here.*

Instead, he found himself asking, "Miss, can I help?"

He followed her into the darkness.

Chapter Three

Vicki Westlake sat on the bottom step, thinking: *I must be upset. In the flash's illumination that man looked like Janos Husaruch. Good Lord! There's a dead body upstairs.*

Through the darkness the voice again questioned, concerned, "Can I help?"

Vicki shakily rose and addressed the taller figure in the shadows, "I don't know what to tell you. Maybe you'd better see for yourself. I've never seen anything like it. I don't know what to do."

"Well, what is it?" the figure asked, perhaps a tad reluctantly.

Vicki started to explain, but instead instructed, "Follow me."

She started swiftly up the stairs, hoping her rush would force the man to follow her. He'd better. She did not want to return to that room alone.

She could hear his footsteps behind her. *Thank God! Maybe. Who is this guy?* She hesitated and he caught up to her as they approached the top landing.

"Miss, don't you think you're being rather mysterious?"

Vicki was tempted to comment that mystery was her profession; somehow this didn't seem the right time.

"I'm sorry," she managed unsteadily. "Please just follow me. Perhaps we can do something...."

She let her voice trail away, afraid she'd lose him if she said too much. Vicki pushed on down the corridor. Maybe because he reminded her of someone she liked, she trusted him, felt he was a square guy. *Why did it have to be so damn dark, even with the intermittent lightning and her flashlight?*

"Couldn't we have a little more light?" came his voice.

"There's no electricity."

"Storm knocked it out?"

Vicki let his comment go. These were not the circumstances for long stories—particularly *this* long story. The last thing that she wanted was to scare him off and be left alone with...what she'd found under the bed.

She hesitated before the door. *Had* she actually closed it behind her? She couldn't remember! Vicki stepped back, her face anguished.

"In there?" he questioned.

"Yes," Vicki managed softly, staring straight ahead.

"Are we going in?'

She was silent.

"Miss?"

"Oh, yes. Just give me a minute," she managed.

He turned her to face him in the light of her flash. *He* does *look like Janos Husaruch. Crazy.*

"What, exactly, is going on here?"

Vicki glanced at the room, then back to him. How do you explain finding a dead man in a house that isn't yours, to a complete stranger—to anyone?!

"If I tell you, you won't believe me," Vicki concluded levelly. "You'll have to see for yourself."

"Let me get this straight. You meet me at the door, panic-stricken; lead me through a dark house; then expect me to plunge into a dark room, not knowing what's in there? Maybe I should be going."

"No, wait, please. I can't handle this alone. It's never happened to me before."

"What's never happened before?!" he shot back exasperated.

Vicki shook her head, frustrated, finally saying, "If I tell you, will you promise to help me?"

"Help you with what? You sound as if you were plotting a murder."

"Not quite."

"No more riddles. What is in that room?"

"A dead body."

"Good-bye."

"No, please, wait. I didn't kill him."

"Then who did? It is your house."

"Well, no."

"What do you mean 'no'? You live here?"

"No, I live in Boston."

"Good-bye."

"Wait! We've got to figure out what to do about this man."

"'We'? Is this a joke?"

"I damn well wish it were."

"Are you sure he's dead?"

"He didn't respond when I pinched him."

"You pinched a dead body?"

"I didn't think he was dead."

"Why would you want to pinch a living man—or do I want to hear about this?"

"Never mind! I'll handle this myself!" Vicki flared, turning away, shoving the door open, regretting every word. Her dignified exit was somewhat marred when she took a flyer over a footstool.

Vicki was sitting on the floor, steaming on the inside, aching on the outside (where she'd landed), when her companion took the flashlight from her and touched her arm to ask, "Where is this body?"

"Under the bed."

"Of course, where else?"

After he helped her up, Vicki instructed, "Hold the flashlight," adding hesitantly, "We'll have to get back down on the floor."

"Why not? What could make these mud-splattered trousers any worse?"

Vicki pulled up the covers, the man shone the flashlight, they both looked at each other.

"That's a dead body," a shaken Janos Husaruch affirmed.

Vicki started to agree, when, close up, by flashlight she burst out, "You really *are* Janos Husaruch!"

"Well, yes. That's true, but..."

"I saw you five, six years ago at Symphony Hall. You were wonderful."

"I'm delighted with your fine musical taste, but..."

"But what are you doing here? With me? I mean that we should end up together, here, the odds must be astronomical."

"I'm sure they are, but do you really think under a bed, facing a corpse is the best place for discussing my talent or the laws of probability? If you don't mind, Miss...?"

"Westlake."

"Miss Westlake, I think we'd be better served moving this discussion to the corridor outside—or at least getting up off the floor. Don't you agree?"

"Oh—yes—of course."

They were outside in a moment, neither one admitting to the other, or to themselves, feeling definite relief at escaping that room. At least the flashlight provided the slight solace of illuminating their conference.

"I don't know what came over me just now," Vicki began, with a swift anxious glance towards the room. "I never babble. Never. At all."

"Miss Westlake, that's really not what needs to be explained. There's a dead body under the bed in that room. Forgive my curiosity, but what the hell is going on here?"

Vicki opened her mouth to speak, closed it, and grimaced before beginning, "This isn't going to be easy to explain."

"I'm not surprised. We'd better just call the police. It's their job, not mine."

"We can't. There isn't any telephone service."

"Of course not. If you're going to live with a dead body, you wouldn't want a telephone around."

"I told you. I don't live here," Vicki impatiently corrected her companion.

"Just visiting the corpse?"

"No. I made a deal with friends that I'd stay in an old dark house all night to prove I wouldn't be frightened silly."

"So talk about astronomical odds. Imagine your coming across not only an old dark house but one with its very own corpse."

"There is no need to be sarcastic," Vicki bit out. "I'm just as flabbergasted as you are."

"Honestly, Miss Westlake, did you make up all of this? I can't help thinking all this sounds like a bad mystery."

"If Vicki Westlake made anything up, it would be a damned good mystery."

36

"Vicki Westlake? Where have I...? Ahh, you wrote *Ill Met By Moonlight.* Wait a minute; what are you doing here?"

"I think I just explained that." Her phrasing was a little abrupt, but her tone softened as she digested his observation, "You read my novel?"

"I guess I read, well, three of them," Janos Husaruch answered, spreading his hands and slightly shrugging, "on midnight trains between concert stops. Is this a gambit to work out the plot of the next one?"

Vicki shook her head, regretful she had to chill his hopeful query.

"I'd certainly never write anything like this. I'm as much in the dark as you. I can't imagine Tim, the friend who has charge of this place, knowing about, the, um..."

"Deceased?"

"Ah, yes."

Then Vicki brightened and suggested, "But it doesn't have to be so bad. We can take your car..."

"Not until someone can extricate it from where I cracked up..."

"Oh, dear."

"That, Miss Westlake, is an understatement."

"Are you all right?" Vicki questioned, now understanding the seriousness of her companion's situation. "Were you hurt?"

"Maybe a bump on the head, mainly my pride," Janos downplayed his experience. "Unfortunately, unless you happen to have a car, we're trapped here."

"Oh, dear."

"I was afraid you'd say that."

"Tim won't pick me up until tomorrow morning. It's part of the arrangement. I accepted a challenge from him and another friend that I could read something terrifying and spend the night without being frightened witless. That's the last time I let David Morrow read Ambrose Bierce."

"'The Suitable Surroundings'?"

"Yes," returned Vicki surprised. "How did you know?"

"You aren't the only author I've enjoyed in between impassioned performances and overstuffed receptions. Still, I've certainly never read anything like the jam we're in tonight. How on earth did your friend happen to come by an abandoned house with a corpse?"

"Tim and another friend are in the real estate business; they own several properties in the Lowell area. That's how he came by the house. Don't ask me about the, um, who is that person, anyway?"

Janos crooked a rueful smile by flashlight, indicating his inability to answer the question.

"Silly of me to ask," Vicki agreed. "I, uh, wonder how he actually, uh, passed on. Could it have been natural causes?"

"Under a bed?"

"I guess not."

"I suppose I could try to walk to another house. I do have some friends living at the end of one of these roads running off the main route, though it's a hike," Husaruch doubtfully offered.

"I don't think that's such a hot idea," Vicki responded. "What if the person, um, responsible for what's in the next room is still around? If we split up, we'll both be vulnerable. Besides, you wouldn't get very far in this storm. Listen to that rain. You could easily get lost, or worse."

Janos Husaruch agreed, relieved: "I'm glad you said that. I don't relish going outside now that the wind and rain seem to have taken up where the lightning left off."

"Lucky us," Vicki glumly quipped, glancing back toward the room, shivering.

"Cold?"

"That and more," Vicki admitted.

"Take my coat, then. It's warm on the inside, even if it's been rained on," Husaruch insisted, pulling off his rain coat, revealing a dark suit, white shirt. and a red tie notable even in this gloom.

Hmm, not only chivalrous, but a snappy dresser, Vicki tried unsuccessfully to calm herself with humor. Still, she was enough herself to protest, "Oh no. What about you? My goodness, after walking up the road, you must be soaked. You're even shaking a little."

Janos Husaruch looked back at the room they had fled and then echoed Vicki's earlier words in a tight voice, "Cold and more."

Vicki found herself sinking back against the wall, but straightened as her companion reached to steady her.

"I'm fine," she waved him back.

Avoiding looking back down the corridor, Janos Husaruch said, his nervousness not quite disguised by attempted levity, "Don't let this suggestion ruin any preconceptions you might have had about my dash and derring-do, but do you think we could get off this floor? I'd be unlimitedly grateful for a strong shot of something."

"So would I, but all I have are the dregs of my coffee in a thermos or some tea in the kitchen."

"Sold."

Vicki reflected it ought to have been funny, even ludicrous, the way they were trying to be witty, when they were actually only a hairsbreadth from screaming down the stairs like Moe, Larry, and Curly. She didn't argue when Husaruch took her arm and fairly trotted them back towards the stairs, saying, "Shall we adjourn our discussion to more felicitous surroundings?"

"A morgue would be more felicitous."

"*C'est entendu.*"

Janos Husaruch added as they almost flew to the stairs, "You may have the stuff of another novel here, Miss Westlake."

"Please. This could only happen in real life. No one would ever believe it in a book."

What a relief it would have been to laugh here, but no matter how hard they tried all their humor seemed to mutate into the death's-head variety.

* * * * * *

Everything was quiet now, except for the wind-haunted rain outside and the wood crackling as the rekindled flames consumed it. Janos had been the fire builder not Vicki. They'd pulled their seats closer to the fireplace for warmth and solidarity, Vicki on the couch and Husaruch in the chair. A large ornate knife with a handle of Balkan design and a blade, bright and shining, of ugly length, lay on the table, its scabbard next to it. Janos told her it was a gift from the Czech family that he had gotten out of Czechoslovakia, which he'd been carrying tonight because the friends he'd been visiting wanted to see it. A disquieting ally against unspoken fears. Water was heating in the kettle hanging from the spit that they'd wordlessly set up. Vicki stared into the flames, trying to organize her mind. She still couldn't adjust. What was going on? She found herself wanting to believe Tim had arranged all this as a joke; however, it seemed unlikely, to say the least, that Tim could have persuaded someone to die or to have, himself, committed murder just to scare her.

And here she was with Janos Husaruch, of all people. To call the circumstances screwy was past all understatement. What should she say to him? Surreptitiously, Vicki glanced at the dark man contemplating the burning wood as if it could clarify the situation for him. There were a few lines around his eyes and mouth that that black and white photo in the paper hadn't captured. His jawline sagged just a little, but he still was easy on the eyes. Vicki swiftly averted *her* eyes, under the circumstances embarrassed at her thoughts.

How could she face this man? How could she ever explain what was going on here? Her understandably battered poise was not strengthened by uneasiness over the possibility that he might detect what she secretly thought of him. *Was* he even the person she thought him to be? Anyway, how the dickens could she be even thinking about squaring his behavior with her past imaginings about him right now?! For Pete's sake, someone lay dead upstairs, and here she was considering the ramifications of her secret crush. Couldn't she give one thought to that poor man? Here she'd criticized and challenged David and Tim for the past three months over their indifference to what had happened in Austria, Czechoslovakia, Poland, and China, but she couldn't even drum up sympathy for a man dead, almost literally in her own back yard. Unfortunately, Vicki drew another parallel between her political arguments and her present situation: the "you could be next" consideration. *How* had *that man died? Why had he died? Could the killer be far off in weather like this?*

"I see a quilt here, Miss Westlake. Would you like it?"

Vicki blinked, startled at the consideration of a clearly strained Janos Husaruch.

He added, "I saw you shudder. It is cold, even with the fire."

Vicki hesitated over revealing the true source of her shudder, but decided it would be wiser to turn back the tension rather than heighten it. She sensed that Janos Husaruch's smile was a little too tight at the moment to further burden him with any grisly conjectures. He was probably silently entertaining her own tormenting thoughts on the reason behind the death in this house. But she had to stay in control.

"I think our tea will be ready soon, Mr. Husaruch. That might take a bit of the chill off both of us. Why are you smiling like that?"

His ruefully amused expression bewildered Vicki, but it also relieved her by provoking curiosity about something other than what they had left upstairs.

Husaruch shook his head, spreading his hands as he explained, "Sorry. It's just all this 'Miss Westlake' and 'Mr. Husaruch', 'Would you like a quilt?' 'Will you have some tea'?—we sound as if we were in Hollywood's version of a British drawing room rather than...this house..."

His voice trailed off a little as Vicki's smile turned into a shudder at the macabre conclusion of his observation.

"I am sorry," he reassured Vicki. "I didn't mean to upset you. I know it's not funny."

"No. I, it's not your fault," Vicki groped. "It's just, well, it just doesn't make any sense—that man being here, dead. And, I, well, I feel responsible."

"You? How?"

He was genuinely surprised and, to Vicki's dismay, a little uneasy at her disclosure. Hastily, she leaned forward to explain, "I don't mean I'm involved. I just mean, I know it's foolish, but I can't help feeling none of this would have happened if I hadn't come here tonight. How could I have any right to play such a silly game in such a serious world? It's not rational, I know, but that's how I feel. Guilty."

Vicki stared into the fire, twisting the fingers of her right hand in the grasp of her left, no longer having a leather watchband to fret. Not only did she feel guilty, but she felt like a grade-A dope. What an ass she was making out of herself, opening up to a stranger. How could she have let down her guard?

"I don't know if this makes you feel any better, but he'd still be dead, whether or not you'd spent the night here," Husaruch carefully pointed out.

Vicki faced him again. His eyes were incongruously dark while still bright with the firelight. At least they were concerned, not judging. Maybe he didn't think she was stupid. Her features relaxed slightly, her eyes warmed. For a moment Vicki felt something kind pass between them. She glanced down at her lap, slightly raising her left hand for emphasis, trying to weaken the spell of this man she did not know. "I guess there is no 'appropriate' way to feel. Who knows? I guess we're both entitled to be a little, oh..."

"Scared?"

Vicki started slightly at his forthright admission before letting the corners of her mouth turn up slightly, surprising herself with, "You're scared, too?"

He cocked his head, surprised at her surprise: "You don't think I could walk in on a corpse on a dark and stormy night and not be? What's so special about me?"

Now it was Vicki's turn to flounder, but not too much. Some hard knocks had left her with better control than that. Still, it could be awkward to discuss another person's personal traumas with him—especially when he was a stranger. Vicki leaned back on the couch, then answered pensively, "You've been through so much, Mr. Husaruch. You, lost your wife, and, just this spring, helped that Czech family escape the Nazis. How many people could outrun a two-day invasion and the occupation of an entire country?"

Husaruch's bitter smile in response surprised Vicki. He tightly replied, "News reports greatly exaggerate. 'Heroes' make better copy than real men, scared men."

Vicki flinched, confused over what nerve she had unintentionally scraped, uncertain whether to be angry with his sharpness or feel guilt over her unintended tactlessness. He read all this on her face with a swift perspicuity that slightly unsettled her.

"I'm sorry, Miss Westlake," he apologized rapidly. His eyes sought hers earnestly: "It's not you with whom I'm angry. It's myself. It's the world. I help one family, out of how many millions, and *I'm* a hero? The real heroes are those people who hid us and helped us to escape routes out of the country. I ran."

"Well, you couldn't possibly have done anything against the Nazis. Look how they infiltrate countries, find out all the government information, put their own people secretly in positions of power, and then they send in the soldiers. They control everything. What could you do? What can...?"

"What can anyone do?" he finished for her bitterly. Husaruch was on his feet, crossing to the fire, folding his arms. "That's what everyone says. Britain and France declare war when it's too late."

"The Germans haven't invaded France yet. Maybe..."

"Maybe they're biding their time."

He faced her, his eyes glittering bitterly in the hearth's light. He turned back to the fire, shaking his head, "You know, I listen to old Senator Borah beef about wasting time and lives and money in foreign entanglements—then I remember what I saw in those Czech villages and in Prague: people rounded up; the scorn, the hatred for the Czechs. I'm not sure how we got out. Being Jewish doesn't make me any fonder of those bastards, either. I don't think you ever can understand until you've seen that hatred and ferocity turned on you, and people like you. Even living across the ocean, I'd been in a cotton-lined existence, caught up in my life as a musician. I hadn't *really* understood it till then."

Husaruch shook his head and walked away from Vicki, back to his chair. It took a few moments for her to notice the kettle shuddering with boiling water, jetting steam. Very quietly, she sighed, thinking about Janos Husaruch's anger and anguish. She knew it wasn't really her he'd flared at, but that realization didn't help her decide what to say next. Well, she was getting to know the man behind the ideal, all right. She couldn't say which she preferred, although she recognized the latter was a lot less painful to deal with. Sometimes you forgot just how messy human relations could be. Her main concern, as she rose to remove the kettle, was how to address Husaruch's angst. She certainly didn't intend to insult him with platitudes. She wasn't going to deny his feelings just so *she* could feel more comfortable. Even tougher for her, she was too much of a soft touch beneath her smart-talking exterior to leave the man brooding over something that, at least for tonight, was beyond the control of either of them.

"Sorry for flying off at you like that."

He had broken the silence. Vicki turned to face him watching her. He wasn't exactly sheepish, but he seemed to genuinely regret his outburst.

"I realize," he continued, "you feel bad enough about the, ah, deceased, upstairs without my forcing you to shoulder the fall of Europe, too. I guess I'm too unnerved to think straight now."

43

Vicki let him off the hook with, "I'm actually on your side. I've had the same argument with too many people to count. But you're right. I can't really know; nobody can really know who hasn't been there. And when you find no one knows or, worse, cares, you want to scream and lash out. I do understand it must be so much worse when you've lived through even a part of it. Anyway, cracking up your car and being stuck in this miserable place with me and a dead man is enough to set anybody off. At least you didn't run out on me."

"In this storm? Are you kidding? After what you showed me under the bed? I'm not going anywhere alone until we're far away from this place—and the person who, ah, disposed of our friend upstairs," Janos responded, trying to be funny, seeming to appreciate Vicki's attempt to soothe him.

Vicki reached for a towel to protect herself from a burn when she removed the hot kettle from the flames, then straightened up and ironically observed to her companion, "You know, I think the only reason neither of us has gone for the obvious and suspected the other is that we're both famous."

Husaruch almost imperceptibly jerked his head with surprise as he digested Vicki's words and broke into probably his first unconstrained smile of the evening to agree, "I'll be damned, you're right."

For the first time in the past few hours, Vicki felt she could smile, too. Only just now did she feel at all safe.

"Tea?" she offered, nodding toward the kettle.

"I'll say. Too bad we haven't anything stronger."

"Sorry. You'll just have to let it steep extra long."

"If I let it steep that long, it'll be able to walk off on its own."

Vicki smiled, pouring the steaming water. At least she had an ally. Against, well, either the deceased or his executioner. She wasn't sure which frightened her more. Too bad that poor dead man hadn't had an ally to help him.

"Thanks."

Janos watched her pouring hot water into his tea, their faces not far apart, neither having actually to meet the other's eyes to enjoy the mutual security they needed in this house turned tomb.

Vicki had stepped back to pour the boiling water into her cup, when Janos praised her lightly, but no less sincerely, "Thank God you kept your head enough to scrounge up these mugs and the tea from the kitchen, and even organize setting up the spit."

"It didn't take an Einstein," Vicki laughed, cutting herself off a little too quickly with a glance toward the stairs beyond the foyer. Still, she was more at ease when she reseated herself to let her tea steep. She liked the way Janos Husaruch's features seemed to welcome her.

"I imagine it's your control and logic that enable you to craft such fine mysteries," Husaruch surmised.

Vicki brightened as the unexpected compliment touched a neglected place in her heart: "I really appreciate your saying that. So many think of creative people as flibbertigibbets. They assume that if you're artistic you have to be impractical, out in left field."

"Hardly. Believe me, I know a true artist needs a tough, strong intellect to harness his creativity," he assured Vicki, indicating his weariness with having to deal with the same prejudices as those bedeviling her.

"Well, thank you. You're really very thoughtful and sensitive. What you said means a lot to me."

"Let's just say I respect your grace under pressure."

"What 'grace'? I made you go into the kitchen to help me. I wasn't going anywhere alone."

"You think I'd stay *here* alone?"

The corners of Vicki's mouth started to turn up but stopped abruptly. She had to admit, "I feel so, I don't know, cold, callous, smiling when that poor man is...."

Vicki ended her dispirited trail of words by staring anxiously, sadly out into the foyer, her hands flattened tensely on her lap.

Husaruch swallowed. His gaze dropped to contemplate his darkening tea. Finally he spoke: "Yes, I know. I sit here thinking I should be outside. Maybe not looking for the murderer but at least trying to get the police—but I don't want to go out there. It could be foolhardy. Dangerous."

"I don't want to go out there, either," Vicki admitted quickly.

Their eyes fell on the knife and, without looking at her, he decided, "I don't want to have to use *that*, either."

"Don't then. I don't want you...to have to," Vicki reassured him. She sat straight and decided for them both, "No more violence."

They anxiously faced each other for what seemed an endless stretch, acutely sensitive to the snapping, devouring fire; the creaking old house; and the spattering of wind-driven rain punctuating the silence.

"We can't leave. We can't do anything, but wait for the morning," Vicki rationally concluded at last.

Janos Husaruch nodded, "You're right. You're logical and correct, Miss Westlake. So why do I feel guilty?"

Vicki shook her head, her mouth twisting, not looking at her companion until she'd finished speaking, "Because we're afraid, too. We hate to admit it. We hate to admit we're helpless."

Husaruch raised his head slightly but sharply enough to reveal that Vicki had struck home. Bouncing his steepled fingers, he admitted, "Like I couldn't really do anything but help one little family. Like Stalin and Hitler and the Japanese, even Mussolini, can do whatever they want, and I can't do anything. We're all helpless."

Vicki really sank inside now. He seemed so pained; and, come to think of it, so was she. From the world beyond U. S. borders to that poor soul upstairs, even her own attempt to prod Tim into doing something with his life, how much control could anybody exert? She couldn't quite look at Janos Husaruch, so she stared into the fire, interlacing her fingers while she thought.

"Mr. Husaruch?"

He only looked at her sideways, still brooding.

"At least that one family is still alive. At least you, and they, can tell people, make people listen. It's not finished yet," she reasoned slowly, subdued but forceful.

"Is this a pep talk?"

"No. It's a 'stop feeling sorry for ourselves' talk. It's a stop being so hubristic you think you're the only one who can change the world—and that 'you' applies to both of us, plural. You did help that family escape—how many people would have just left alone, taken care of only number one? And I can lead a real estate agent to romance, but I can't make him do what will make him happy. Don't look so bewildered; it's a long story about my friends Tim and Sunny, and you don't want to know. Let's face it: neither one of us is Sherlock Holmes. We can't nab a murderer, so let's leave it to the pros. What we can do when we leave here is tell the police everything we know—and you can continue with your benefits for war relief. Me—well, I'll think of something."

"Miss Westlake, you *are* something."

"For heaven's sake; it's not as if you just heard Eleanor Roosevelt," Vicki insisted, not completely successful in camouflaging her appreciation with a no-nonsense mien.

"No, maybe not the first lady, but you are a great deal like another important woman I knew. She could look you in the eye and call a spade a spade, but still make you feel good about yourself, no matter how angry she was with you."

"Who is that?"

"Well, perhaps I can tell you later. I just think, Miss...may I call you Vicki? Under the circumstances, all this formality is starting to seem ludicrous."

"Oh, um, yes. All right."

Vicki found herself growing less successful at checking the camaraderie he evoked in her.

"Vicki, I just thought you should know that I like you. I know I may sound a bit forward, and maybe a little odd under the present circumstances. But I've always been forthright. Then again, spontaneity brought Barbara and me together." He smiled to himself, reflecting on that past meeting. "At any rate, you have a sharp mind and a good heart. I think I always believed that you'd be this kind of person."

Vicki blinked, startled at this unexpected admission from the man across from her.

"You...always...thought? About me? You don't know me. How? We know nothing, really nothing, about each...well, we never met till tonight."

Janos tipped his head a little awkwardly to the side, leaning back into his chair a bit self-consciously and countered, "I guess so, but you know, Vicki, I don't think any artist can create without infusing his piece with part of his soul. You have some pretty hair-raising plots, but I notice that your characters are mainly concerned with being responsible for others. Not a fear of social unacceptability, but a caring—a caring about being

47

humane, and being ethical. Always, I've said to myself, here's a woman with a good heart. Here's someone I could like."

"You thought that? About *me*?"

Vicki's words were slow; one corner of her mouth crept up, beyond her control. Beyond her control was the delighted amazement that blocked out every anxiety of the past few hours, even the cynicisms of the past few years. He was nodding, his smile invitingly meeting hers. Janos Husaruch seemed almost poised to move nearer her, just waiting for her signal.

She was so close to letting slip some of her own secret thoughts, almost willing to risk vulnerability—but she couldn't. She would not. Experience had taught her the value of being careful. She waited for what he would say next, waiting out this hand with hope in her heart.

He hesitated, then took a chance: "Once we're out of this place, would you like to meet again, under better circumstances?"

Vicki started to brighten; but she caught herself. *Wolves. The wounded ones, the two-legged kind, are the worst.* How did she know there wasn't something hungry and fanged lurking under that sheep's "gosh, you're swell" act of the past few minutes?

No, she didn't know for certain it was an act; but she did know it was too damned good to be true that Janos Husaruch should harbor a crush of sorts on her. True, a deserted mansion, downstairs from a corpse, oughtn't have been the most felicitous of situations for a come-on. Still, years of knowing too many fast-talking guys, and being jilted by a fella she'd let herself trust, had clued her in to the unsavory fact that even tonight's unfavorable conditions could prove an irresistible challenge to some men. Husaruch had lived in Europe for years, probably traveled in some fast artistic circles on two continents—and she was just a home-grown girl from Massachusetts. No, after all she'd been through, particularly with the guy she'd been lucky enough *not* to marry, Vicki Westlake knew better than to put anything past anyone, no matter how much she wanted to believe in people.

That train of thought seared Vicki in a split second; leaving Janos Husaruch disoriented when she compressed her features into a somber chill and distantly replied, "Yes, well, I'll think about it. These are hardly the circumstances for me to be playing Public Debutante Number One."

Vicki berated herself for internally wincing at her companion's confused expression. Still, he could just be a good actor. Anyway, how could she possibly leave herself vulnerable to someone she knew so little about?

"Ah, fine. I'm sorry. I didn't mean to overstep my bounds."

He gave her a quick, uncertain glance, then contemplated his tea, sourly crooking his mouth.

Vicki licked her lower lip, feeling like the back end of a shoe, a real heel. But she refused to let on how she felt. She didn't know him. She'd tap-danced her way out of too many fast-talkers' traps to let a schoolgirl crush bring her down now.

"Too bad we don't have sugar cubes. I remember watching my father drink his tea with a cube clenched in his teeth," he began in an attempt to restore their camaraderie. "Very old world. He was Hungarian but grew up in the Ukraine, where he met my mother. He brought her and my older sister over here before I was born. To Shifra, my younger brother and I were the spoiled American brats. Now I get even by spoiling her two children. They're the spoiled Americans now."

Vicki folded her hands and stared at her tea. This evening was getting worse and worse, if things *could* go downhill after finding a dead man. Either she was being an unmitigated stinker or she was stuck alone with someone, if he was sleazy enough to put the moves on her under these circumstances, who might or might not get forceful about dishonorable intentions. She couldn't win, right or wrong. And there was that knife on the table.

Wearily, Vicki leaned her forehead into her upraised hand, braced against the arm of the couch. Her sigh, almost a groan, was unsuppressible.

"I am sorry. I forgot what a strain all this must be on you." Husaruch seemed almost relieved to have found an excuse for her coldness. "Would you like me to fix your tea?"

Vicki hesitated, looking at him carefully. She always had been a sucker for solicitude. But she still didn't know him.

"No thank you. I'm fine."

She quickly leaned forward and pulled out the tea bag, adding the sugar, while coolly ignoring him, even though she inwardly tensed at sensing him study her.

"You didn't think I was coming on to you? That's not it?"

A trifle nettled at the surprise in his tone (was he implying she wasn't worth it or that she was over-reacting?), Vicki smoothly returned, "It wouldn't be the first time."

She reclined against the couch like a watchful cat, holding her mug, in control.

"Don't you think the circumstances are a bit, shall we say, macabre, for that sort of thing?"

Was he amused at her? Taking measured sips, Vicki gazed regally past him, as if intrigued by the much more fascinating shadows beyond and tossed off, "I don't put much past anyone these days." Focusing directly on him, "I don't really know you."

He smiled ruefully and looked down at his tea, agreeing, "No, I guess you don't." Looking back up at Vicki, he added, "But I'm sorry you've had experiences to make you bitter."

That rattled Vicki, because for a warm and dangerous split second, she believed he *was* sorry. Abruptly, she returned the mug to the table, splattering some dead person's furniture. On her feet, Vicki impatiently adjusted her belt as she walked to the fireplace and informed her companion, "Don't be so sorry. I'm just fine, thank you." Turning to face him, she finished, "I'm not exactly an old lady living alone with thirty cats."

"I didn't say you were," he uttered, a little overwhelmed.

Vicki caught herself, embarrassed to realize she was overreacting. Being jilted, then that summer with David, and all the other of her disappointments, none of those were Husaruch's fault. But it *was* scary to recognize she'd let her defenses down with him before she really knew him.

Vicki looked into the fire and allowed without apologizing "It's been a long night. I'm tired. Ho, I'll be glad when this is over."

"Both of us will. We're entitled to be on edge, considering where we are and who may still be around. At any rate, if you can listen to me rant about the fall of Europe, I can listen to you..."

"*I* wasn't ranting," Vicki corrected, turning sharply to face Husaruch, her eyes narrowing.

"No, I guess I was the grandstander. At least loneliness is something natural to everyone..."

"I'm not lonely," Vicki shot back.

Janos Husaruch surprised her by laughing, "You may not be, but I am." Then he was sober, "I'd give anything to have Barbara, my late wife, back. Isn't there someone about whom you feel that way?"

"No," Vicki insisted, a little too sharply. Upset that he had seen more about her than she wanted him to, Vicki cast herself as too tough to get hurt anymore, "I'll tell you, there was someone, someone I almost married. But it was too much trouble for him to stick around. Life was just too uncertain for him to stick to long range plans—he claimed. So that was that, and here we are in this hideous house."

That's when the boards overhead creaked torturously. For an infinitesimal fraction of a second, they stared terrified at each other, a hairsbreadth from leaping forward like two frightened children and grabbing each other for protection. The wind snarled furiously around the house.

Vicki turned abruptly, breaking the spell, returning to the couch with, "The house is settling under the wind. It's only the house settling. That's all."

"Ah, certainly, of course," Husaruch agreed, not facing her. "If I'd killed someone, I certainly wouldn't hide out in the same place, even in this weather."

"Although a murderer wouldn't have any way of knowing there'd be people here. It would just be a deserted old house to anyone but my friends and me," Vicki speculated with growing disquiet.

"Could we change the subject, Miss Westlake?" Janos proposed, nervously getting up. "If we have to ride out the storm here, I could do without any conjectures like those."

Vicki started to speak. Yes, she was terrified. She wanted to cry. But she would *not* admit it. She just dropped her eyes and gnawed away the last vestige of her Max Factor.

"Miss Westlake, I am sorry I've upset you. But please, don't be angry. I really would like to talk with you once we're out of this place."

Vicki looked up. The words had tumbled out of him and he seemed so earnest now. She wanted to apologize, too; wanted to lay to rest some old ghosts. After all, it would only be talking. But the unexpected realization that their both being famous was a flimsy excuse to clear either of them of murder jostled her momentum. How could she be so naive?

"I..," he began, only to be interrupted by a pounding on the front door. Vicki nearly jumped out of her skin.

"What the hell!" she heard Janos Husaruch utter. His eyes were no less startled than hers when he demanded, "Who is it?"

"How would I know," she replied, softly, anxiously, eyes fastened on the doorway beyond. "I only came here to be terrified."

"You'd better answer it," Janos Husaruch prompted.

"Me?!" Vicki shot back, her dismayed gaze switching to her companion. "I don't think so."

"*We'd* better answer it," he decided, rising. He jested shakily, "It's silly to worry. I'd hardly expect a murderer to knock."

"Unless he was reporting to Lord and Lady Macbeth," Vicki muttered, though not terribly amused by the situation.

The knocking grew more insistent.

"We need to answer it," Janos Husaruch reiterated, looking from Vicki into the darkness of the corridor, but still not moving. "It could be our ticket out of here."

Vicki reached down and as she straightened up, explained, "I have the flashlight."

"Good. Maybe I'll just grab the knife," Janos added, slipping the knife into his suit coat's inside pocket.

Vicki silently, nervously nodded.

The knocking continued, whether angrily or anxiously, neither could quite tell. They looked at each other. Perhaps with a touch of defiance, Vicki switched on the flashlight and, before Janos could take the lead, pushed past him into the corridor. Nervousness couldn't entirely supplant her determination not to appear weak.

"Vicki? Are you in there? Is everything all right?"

At the sound of that anxious inquiry from outside, Vicki pulled the door open and blurted out forcefully, "Thank God you're here. You wouldn't believe what I found in the bedroom upstairs."

At these words, Vicki's guests discerned Janos Husaruch stepping out of the shadows.

"Hmm, Tim, you *do* think of all the comforts. Who'll be in my haunted house, Lana Turner?" mused David.

"Who's this?" Tim cut in startled, even displeased.

"Janos Husaruch," Janos identified himself quickly.

"Oh yes, I thought you looked familiar. You're the one Vicki, ah, respects as a musician," David affably observed, his change of wording noticeable only to Vicki. Maybe he was a good friend, after all, not mentioning *everything* she'd admired.

"Yes," Vicki added. "These are my friends, Mr. Husaruch. David Morrow and Tim West. They must be here to check up on me!"

"Wonderful to meet you both. Now why don't we all dash out to your car and hurry into Lowell and get the police?"

"Police? What have you two kids been up to?" David chided with a maddening twinkle.

"David, this is no joke," Vicki warned authoritatively. "I found a dead body upstairs in the bedroom."

"And where did you find your friend? I love it when your eyes flash like that, you vixen," David teased.

Janos Husaruch stepped forward, allaying some of Vicki's ire by interjecting, "Mr. Morrow, when you take us to the Lowell police you can hear the entire story. Let's stop wasting time."

"Mr. Husaruch, you can't tell us there's a dead body upstairs and not expect us to be curious. Where did you find it?" David persisted.

"I told you, in the bedroom," Vicki snapped. "Under the bed. Is that specific enough for you? Now can we go?"

"There's a corpse under the bed and you want us to go? This we must see. Right, Tim?"

"You need help to look?" Janos remarked.

"Tim is a real estate agent. This is his house," David returned easily.

"Perhaps your friend ought to inspect his property more often," Janos cracked.

"I don't often have to worry about corpses under beds," Tim, who had been sourly silent at Husaruch's presence, finally spoke.

The two stared each other down for a moment.

"This is silly, wasting time," Vicki interposed. "Let's go."

"Right," agreed David, grabbing Vicki's flashlight and bounding up the stairs.

Vicki stood, furiously stunned at David's departure up the stairs, an exit copied by Tim. She had just fixed her eyes on a likely object to throw at them when Janos Husaruch put a hand on her arm and pointed out, "Remember how I reacted when I first saw the body?"

In spite of herself, Vicki smiled.

"And you would love to see their expressions, wouldn't you?" Janos inquired as he took the knife from his suit coat's inner pocket.

"David, please wait for us," Vicki called sweetly.

"Just give me a minute to put the knife back in the scabbard and stow it in back my jacket, then you'll have a well-deserved treat," Janos promised.

"All right, but step on it. I don't want to miss a minute of this," Vicki pronounced, champing at the bit.

When Janos and Vicki caught up to her friends on the floor above, David queried, "Aren't you afraid, Vicki?"

"Aren't you?" she sweetly challenged.

"Hmmm," they both laughed with forced smiles at each other.

"Let's not waste time," said Tim peremptorily, snatching the flashlight from David and striding off.

David pivoted and in a few long, quick strides caught up with Tim, who did not slow for Vicki and Janos. Instead, Tim unobtrusively distanced himself from everyone but David so he could say only so his friend could hear, "I don't like this. This Janos Whoever being here."

"Relax, Tim. It's just one more person to get hysterical. Vicki certainly is something less than poised right now."

"He throws off the entire plan."

"Improvise. We all have to. You'd be surprised how well it works."

"Odd talk from Mr. Meticulous, himself," Tim grumbled.

"What are you two talking about?" Vicki demanded, almost upon her two friends now.

David paused, offered a winning smile, and kidded, "Getting a little testy, Vicki?"

"You don't believe us?" she countered, affronted.

"Let's just say I'm skeptical."

"Your other friend seems more annoyed than skeptical, Vicki," Janos noted as he and Vicki closed with Tim and David.

Tim shot Husaruch an irritated glance.

David gestured mock surrender, granting, "Tim hates to find out he has nonpaying tenants."

"Especially dead ones. It's harder to collect back rent," Tim added casually.

"That's disgusting, both of you. A man is dead," Vicki insisted, incredulous at their flippancy. "Don't you even care?"

"If we didn't, would we be here now?" David smoothly inquired.

Vicki and Janos shared disbelieving gazes, but when they turned back to chastise David's callousness, he had left them to join Tim before the terrible door.

The four paused there. They looked at one another. Vicki noted a touch of tension in David's flash-lit features and Tim's as well. *Maybe they weren't so smug?*

"Well? Are you going in?" she demanded of her "rescuers," focusing some of her dread into antagonism toward the men who had gotten her into this fine mess and who seemed so unconcerned about that poor, dead soul.

"Ladies first."

How could David be so damn chipper?

"The lady *was* first," Janos corrected smoothly. "I, the guest, was second. Now it's your turn, gentlemen."

Vicki smiled, just a shadow, and found herself edging a tad closer to Janos. Now Tim looked in control and David seemed almost edgy.

"I think, Vicki, you're probably mistaken. The night plays tricks," Tim seemed to tease. Before she could respond, he nonchalantly opened the door and sauntered into the darkness.

"Join us, kids? Or do you plan to hold hands in the balcony?" David needled before he, too, disappeared into the room.

The two hung back at first, but Vicki squared her shoulders and returned to the unwelcome semi-darkness of that room. Janos hurriedly caught up to her.

Tim stood at the end of the bed, beaming his flashlight about the room, remarking as they entered, "I don't see any corpses, Vicki."

David, standing next to the near side of the bed pointed out helpfully, "She said it was under the bed."

"Ah," Tim agreed, coming around to David.

He knelt down, positioned the flashlight on the floor, then tossed back the hanging spread. Vicki shuddered.

"Hmm," Tim uttered, noncommittally, as he peeked beneath the bed. He reached under and began to blithely pull something out. But he didn't finish.

"Omigod! He's dead!"

Tim leaped back, trembling. Still crouching, he goggled at Vicki and Janos to stammer, "He's dead. Really dead."

"I believe that's what Miss Westlake and I have been trying to tell you," Janos countered, not quite as coolly as he would have liked.

"But he's not supposed to be dead," Tim blurted.

"What?" Vicki demanded piercingly.

"There's not supposed to be a real corpse here. What are we going to do?"

"What do you mean there's not supposed to be a 'real' corpse?" Vicki pressed threateningly.

David cut in before Tim could respond, "Tim, why do I have the feeling that your little gag has gotten way out of hand?"

"Because it has, damn it! He wasn't supposed to die! I didn't pay him to die!"

"Pay whom? What are you two up to?" Vicki insisted. "What is this rat I smell?"

Janos Husaruch leaned back against the wall and shook his head, thinking out loud, "I should have stayed in the car. Ditch, rain, lost—I'd have been much safer. Maybe I have a concussion and this is all a dream."

"What do I do? David? How did he die?"

"Why are you asking me, Tim? I didn't plot this scheme, hire this man. It's *your* ball game."

"Hire? Timothy, what did you do?" Vicki flared. "What is going on here."

Vicki had grabbed the bewildered Tim West by the lapels, so that Janos had to step in, saying, "All right. Wait. We can all get a nice, lucid explanation on the way to the police station. The last thing this house needs now is not *another* corpse, however justified you may feel homicide to be at the moment, Miss Westlake. Why don't we all get into your friends' car and leave here while we can?"

Janos Husaruch's rhetorical question was answered by a sickening skidding sound followed by the impact of metal on metal outside the house.

Momentarily, all four people stared at each other, then Tim, David, and Vicki rushed from the room, leaving Janos Husaruch alone. Looking about his less-than-warm surroundings, Janos mused, "Why do I have the feeling that a car crash was the answer to my questions?"

Whether from curiosity or fear, Janos all but sprinted out of the room after the others.

Despite their long strides, David and Tim soon found themselves distanced by Vicki Westlake and her flashlight's head start. Two steps from the top of the lower landing, Vicki brought the caravan to an abrupt halt. Her flashlight caught the back of a woman in a green raincoat and black kerchief closing the front door, working flashlight in hand. Vicki's suspicions were confirmed when her light provoked the intruder to turn, startled.

"Sunny!" came Tim's incredulous voice from behind Vicki.

Vicki froze in shock as Sunny's expression flashed from alarm to fury.

"That was your car I skidded into?" Sunny accused.

"How bad is it?" ventured Tim.

Ignoring him, she questioned, "What are you doing here?" Anxiously, "Is anyone else here?"

"Funny you should ask," David mused awkwardly.

Sunny blanched. She managed tentatively, almost as if fearing the answer, "Who else?"

Everyone on the stairs looked uncomfortably at each other. Sunny approached the foot of the stairs. Her hand crushingly gripped the decorative rail post.

"Who is it?"

"More like, who *was* it," David corrected.

"That's tactful," Vicki muttered. She wasn't prepared, though, for the horror in Sunny's eyes and the woman's furious dash past them, up the stairs, and round the corner.

Completely at a loss, the four stood staring at one another. Finally Janos Husaruch dryly noted, "Interesting friends you have here, Miss Westlake."

Before Vicki could reply, she was silenced by Sunny's scream.

"Oh, my god," Vicki uttered, pushing past the dumbfounded men to get to her friend.

Vicki found Sunny on the far side of the bed. Her disconsolate friend was kneeling by the upper half of the body that she had managed to pull from under the bed. Sunny swayed, mindlessly repeating, "No, no, no."

"Sunny. It's Vicki. I'm here. What is happening? Please, let me help," Vicki said slowly, quietly, sinking down next to her friend, fighting the revulsion of being near the dead man.

Sunny could only drag an anxious hand across her face and insist, "It can't be. It can't be. Not him. Not now."

"What, Sunny? Who is he? What's wrong?" Vicki persisted gently. "Talk to me. Who is he?"

The three men reached the room in time to hear Sunny answer blankly, "He's the man for whom I was going to leave my husband."

Surprisingly, Sunny was the only one to faint after that revelation.

Chapter Four

The study was spacious and booklined. It was also fairly dark and dreary, illuminated, along with its three occupants, only by the nascent fire in the hearth. Sunny lay on the couch slightly to the side of the fire, where David had gently placed her after carrying her from the bedroom upstairs. Vicki sat in a chair by her friend's side, holding the unconscious woman's hand, not sure why they were here rather than the parlor, not even sure whose idea it had been to come in here. David was endeavoring to strengthen the fire in the hearth that was located opposite the doors. Tim was in the kitchen, from whence he had promised to bring the proper materials for tea.

Vicki's gaze drifted from her friend to Janos Husaruch. He stood by the wall, off to her right, beyond the couch. He studied Sunny intently. Funny how he seemed so concerned for a woman he didn't know. Had she been too hard on him with her earlier suspicions?

"No!"

Sunny sat up abruptly, nailing Vicki's attention. David stood up and approached.

"It's all right, Sunny," Vicki soothed.

"No, it can't be. He's dead. Murdered."

"Murdered?" Vicki echoed. True, she and Janos Husaruch had both pretty much drawn the same conclusion, but, somehow, coming from Sunny....

"Yes! Murdered!"

"But who? Why?" Vicki questioned quietly.

"Jealousy?" proposed David. "Bob, maybe?"

Sunny looked at him hard a moment, then down at her hands before saying, "Yes, Bob."

"But Bob's in Havana," Vicki protested.

Sunny smiled bitterly, "Maybe yes, maybe no. Some of Bob's Havana trips were to a woman in Sandwich."

"Ho! That rat. How dare he two-time you?" Vicki burst out.

Ruefully, Sunny replied, "But I can cheat on him?"

Vicki looked down embarrassed. Finally, she managed, "But he was first, I'm sure. Oh, and, Sunny, Bob made you so unhappy. He hurt you. I saw it."

"Two wrongs don't make a right," Sunny pointed out steadily.

"Well, it's not as if you did this all the time. You wanted to marry your, ah, fellow," Vicki insisted.

Sunny looked at her friend strangely, almost uncomfortably, then looked away, only to be startled by the sight of Janos.

He swiftly introduced himself, more than a little awkwardly, "I am Janos Husaruch. Of course you don't know me."

Sunny stared at him a moment, displeased, before looking at Vicki to muse ruefully, "You're having quite a party here."

"Complete with a corpse," David pointed out before he realized what he'd said.

Sunny was stricken. Vicki shot up and demanded, "Damn it, David. How can you be this insensitive? Why don't you take a walk, preferably until your hat floats."

"Please! Stop! I just want to be alone," Sunny burst out, her head buried in her hands.

Vicki quietly sat beside her friend, but Sunny didn't seem to see her. Looking up, Vicki was surprised to see Tim watching them from the doorway, his expression revealing that his feelings for Sunny hadn't changed. Vicki's heart ached, especially after Sunny's revelation about the man upstairs. Especially after what she, herself, had urged earlier this evening. Why hadn't Sunny married the right man: Tim who would never dream of hurting her?

Perceiving Vicki's thoughts, Tim blanked his features, quietly stating, "I think Sunny's right. Why don't we leave her alone for now?"

Sunny had lain back on the couch, her arm blocking them all out. The other three friends exchanged questioning looks, but Tim's quiet, controlled expression prompted them to move into the foyer. Vicki squeezed Sunny's shoulder before leaving.

Tim closed the doors behind them, as David questioned, "So, Tim, why a pow-wow in the foyer?"

Slowly, Tim began, "Sunny is right. That man was murdered."

"Really, Charlie Chan? What makes you so sure?"

Ignoring David's sarcasm, Tim explained, "I've been upstairs, not just fixing tea in the kitchen. I looked...at the body. The man's Adam's apple was crushed and there were horrific bruises on his neck. He didn't accidentally tie his tie too tight. You don't have to be Charlie Chan to sniff out a crime here."

"And someone clearly didn't want the body found. Not just left in a deserted house, but hidden in it," Janos Husaruch surmised.

"Looks like this is right up your alley, Vicki," David concluded darkly.

"I don't think this is quite the time, David," Vicki responded coolly, not bothering to look at her friend. She continued, "Can you tell how long the man has been dead, Tim?"

"I'm not a coroner, Vicki," he answered, but not sarcastically. "But the body isn't that cold and it certainly hasn't decomposed."

They all stood silently in the flickers of the firelight leaking into the foyer from the living room. No one *wanted* to ask what to do next. It was Vicki who began, "Do you think the murderer is still around?"

"He couldn't have proceeded far if he killed after the storm started," Janos extrapolated.

"But we don't know when this man was killed. We don't even know for certain who the murderer is," Vicki pointed out, frustrated.

"Sunny had an idea," David disagreed.

"Who?" Tim perked up.

"Bob, of course," David returned matter-of-factly. "She said as much a moment ago."

Tim eyed his friend skeptically, while Vicki disagreed, "Sunny's hysterical. How can we trust what she's saying?'

"You trust Bob? Who else had a motive, Vicki?" David reasoned.

"How would Bob know where to find her or what was going on?" she argued, a touch fiercely.

"There are such things as private detectives," pressed David, undaunted.

Vicki began to snap back, but decided against it for Sunny's sake. She was pleased to hear Janos Husaruch articulate her thoughts: "Any louder and we might as well walk back into the study and argue in front of your friend."

Before David could get the last word, Tim agreed, "Mr. Husaruch is right. We can't stand here and bicker. All I wanted to do was make you aware of the facts. I hoped we could take better care of ourselves and calm Sunny. Keep her from going back up there. Relax her until the storm lets up, and then we can contact the authorities. Sunny should be our main concern—"

"Excuse me, Tim, but if there's a murderer around, I think I have the right to be concerned about myself, too," David corrected.

"We can best take care of all ourselves," Janos calmly pointed out, "if we sit tight here and wait out the storm. There is no reason for us to do otherwise."

Tim's sage nod of agreement was interrupted by Sunny's scream from beyond the study doors. Janos might have missed at least one reason to feel safe here.

When the four burst into the study, Sunny stood trembling, staring at the rain-lashed windows a few feet from her, looking out of the front of the house.

"Sunny, what is it?" Vicki questioned, reaching the other woman's side, her relief indescribable that her friend was all right.

"The face. Oh, God, the face," Sunny managed. Then, turning to Vicki, Sunny calmed only slightly when she elaborated, "I thought I heard scratching at the window. I was sure it was the rain, but it kept up—like a person, a person's nails. And then I got up and saw the face."

"All right, all right," Vicki comforted, bringing her friend back to the couch.

"Was it Bob?" David questioned.

"Can't you give it a rest?" snapped Tim as he moved to sit beside Sunny.

"You don't believe me, do you?" Sunny pressed Tim.

"It's not a question of that," Tim assured her gently.

"Isn't it? You all think I'm hysterical. I don't think any of you believe I saw someone," she accused, looking hard at each of them.

"It's not a question of disparaging you," Vicki tried to soothe.

Sunny was not in the least soothed. She countered, "What is it a question of? Even after all these years holding the office together, you still don't really see me as capable, do you? Any of you? David asked a good question. If that was Bob, I could be next. He must have killed Jon. Who else would have? He was jealous. With him, what was good for the gander wasn't at all o.k. for the goose. That's why Jon and I had to meet on the sly, until I could get a divorce; but Bob must have found out, somehow. And he killed Jon. Now he wants to kill me. But not one of you believes me."

"I believe you," Tim assured Sunny.

"Do you? Do you really, Tim?" Sunny questioned seriously. "Then will you go out there and find him, or at least make sure he's not around?"

"Sunny," argued Vicki, "there's a horrible storm out there. Listen to that wind and rain. I know there are more flashlights, but I don't know if there are enough to go around. It's too dangerous."

"I've set up some hurricane lamps in the kitchen," Tim countered, pondering.

"Timothy West, you're not thinking about going out there," Vicki countered.

"Vicki's right," David began reasonably. "It's dark, pouring rain; you don't know where this character is hiding. Whether you find him or not, Tim, you lose. He certainly won't waltz into custody because you asked him politely, and if you don't find him—"

"Or if he finds me?" Sunny cut in. "He will finish me."

"Miss," Janos began, "if we all remain with you, there's no reason he should be able to hurt you. He'll be outnumbered."

"Yes, *now* I'm safe, but if he gets away I may never be. He'll be free and I'll never be secure." She turned to Tim and pleaded, "Tim, I could always rely on you, more than any of the others. My life depends on *you*. I need *you*, Tim. Will you help me?"

Tim didn't say anything. He just stood up and crossed to the foyer. The others were stunned. Finally, Vicki managed, "Tim, wait."

Her words galvanized everyone but Sunny. They pursued Tim into the foyer, where he was busy throwing on his coat.

"You've got to be crazy," David began, spreading his hands in frustration.

"No, just loyal," Tim returned, not even bothering to look at David while lighting the hurricane lamp he had picked up from the floor where he'd lined up three along the wall.

"Mr. West, this isn't logical," Janos calmly disagreed. "You cannot safely find the man by yourself."

"Mr. Husaruch, this isn't your responsibility. Don't worry or interfere."

"Tim, that wasn't fair," Vicki chided.

"Fair or not, I'm sticking by Sunny—whether or not any of you do."

Before the point could be argued further, Timothy West was out the door, hurricane lamp in hand.

Vicki stepped toward the closed door, then turned back to her companions and decided, "We've got to go after him. Help him, bring him back. We can't leave him out there alone."

"Nothing doing, Vicki," argued David. "We can't go out in that. It's too dangerous. With the rain and dark we won't be able to see Bob—or whoever—to catch him, never mind avoid getting hurt."

"Never mind that, Mr. Morrow," Janos Husaruch interjected, "we cannot leave your friend alone—precisely for the reasons you stated. Even if no one's out there, your friend should not be left to wander alone in a storm like this. From the way this Jon was killed, it looks as if the husband, if he's out there, isn't armed, but we need to stick together. There should be safety in numbers."

Vicki regarded Janos thankfully. She wondered if he'd reassure David by revealing that his knife would protect them, but that was his call. Instead, she only seconded him, "You know he's right, David. Tim will be in a real jam, alone out there. Even if Sunny just imagined seeing someone, Tim's too upset to be by himself in this storm. You know that's the truth."

David gave her a dissatisfied smile but conceded, "Yes, you're right. Damn that Tim."

"He thought he was helping your friend," Janos pointed out quietly.

"I guess I can't be any less of a friend," David relented. "All right. Let's go."

"Wait, in case you're worried, you gents should each take a poker, for protection," Vicki suggested. "What do you think?"

"Good idea, kid," David nodded. "And I feel a lot better that you'll be safe in here and keeping an eye on Sunny. See if you can calm the poor kid down."

Janos concurred concerning the pokers, still not mentioning the knife. Well, the poker would work better if they weren't in close quarters, a situation both men would love to avoid, she was sure.

While David dashed into the parlor to grab two pokers, Janos surprised Vicki by taking her aside and saying, "I just wanted you to know I think you'll be a great help to Sunny. I honestly think she needs you."

"You seem to know her so well for a stranger," Vicki noted carefully, not entirely pleased with feeling a ghost of suspicion.

"I'm not patronizing you."

"You shouldn't," Vicki cooly warned, though she wanted to believe him in spite of herself.

"I wouldn't. I've seen enough of that temper and sharp tongue in the past few hours to know better."

His eyes smiled at those words and she caught a smile creeping into her own features. Vicki wouldn't quite look at him, but she could sense he perceived that he'd defused most of her reservations. There was no hostility in her voice when she changed the subject, "Here's David, back with your weapons. Be careful out there, fellas. Hurry back safe. We've had enough casualties this evening."

Janos nodded and drew his lips into a slight smile of agreement before taking his hat and coat from the wall rack and handing David his own.

Vicki watched Janos quietly as he and David quickly checked their hurricane lamps. Serious and intent, Janos looked older. Unexpectedly, he looked up and assured her with surprisingly gentle sincerity, "We'll bring back your friend. Don't worry about him."

"I know you'll do your best. Take care, both of you."

Her own quiet warmth surprised Vicki, but curiously not him. Janos smiled, almost a little eagerly, nodded, and was gone. David regarded Vicki curiously for a moment, before warning, "Lock this door. I don't want anything happening to you, or Sunny." Then he dashed out into the night himself.

65

Vicki could still feel the cold and damp on her face after she closed the door. She could still feel the funny kind of warmth from Janos's candid, calm smile, too. This time she couldn't quite smother her emotions with cynicism. And David's injunction had conveyed a concern that seemed to blast away all his past sarcasm.

About to lock the door, she was interrupted by Sunny's call, "Vicki?"

She turned sharply back to the study. Now how could she have forgotten her friend in this tight spot?

"Coming, Sunny!"

Walking quickly into the study, Vicki found Sunny reclining on the couch, her arms folded, her face clouded in the firelight.

Pulling a comforter over her friend's knees, Vicki queried as comfortingly as she could, "Feeling any better? Warm enough with the blanket and the fire?"

Sunny turned her attention from the firelight to the friend standing before her and questioned quietly, "Did they go out to find Bob?"

Vicki was unsettled by a hardness in her friend's expression that she could never remember seeing in all their years together. Could someone be traumatized into such hardness in one night, or had Sunny been able to hide this part of herself all this time? She'd hidden the lover, or, recalling Sunny's reaction to an earlier remark, Vicki wondered if she should say "lovers." All those thoughts comprised just a brief hesitation before Vicki answered sharply, "Yes, they're out there."

Vicki crossed her arms, against the cold of the house and her friend's eyes.

Calmly defiant, Sunny pressed, "You don't approve. You think I was selfish to send them out."

Vicki looked down at Sunny and was surprised, even a little irritated to see accusation in her friend's eyes. *Bite your tongue*, Vicki cautioned herself. *Sunny's been through so much. How would you feel if the person you loved had been brutally taken from you by a man who had hurt and humiliated you?* Vicki didn't like the fact that a shivery flash of concern for someone out in the storm answered that question. She sank to the footrest before the fire, her eyes straying into the flames.

"Answer my question. You think I'm selfish."

Vicki flashed an angry glance at Sunny, then guiltily tried to soothe her, "You've had a terrible experience, Sunny. Nobody thinks straight under these conditions."

"And now you're patronizing me."

Again Vicki bit her tongue before answering, "No, Sunny. I don't know why you're attacking me, though. I'm sorry for what's happened to you, but I'm worried about David and Tim and—"

"Your new boyfriend? What a stroke of luck for you! The man of your dreams shows up to sweep you off your feet, with the murder of my Jon to bring you two together. The man I truly loved is dead and you get to make cow eyes at some smoothie musician. How lovely for you."

"That's a nasty thing to say," Vicki retorted, shocked, as she rose and stared down at her friend. Her fists slowly clenched.

"Oh, excuse me for treading on tender feelings, Vicki. I've only lost the only man I really loved to another man who took some of the best years of my life and threw them in my face, laughing. Maybe I'm tired of being the sunshine girl for all of you. Maybe I'm entitled to get angry and nasty. You haven't cornered the market on cynicism. Time changes your perspective, rots away what's beneath the surface. I'd like to know what you really know about heartache and hurt—and don't tell me about that fiancé. One disappointment and you think you see through every man; you think you've seen it all. You don't know hurt and bitterness and anger like I do. You don't know—"

"I know not to use my friends. You played Tim like a virtuoso. You knew you could manipulate him into going out there. But you didn't care that you could get him killed. What an actress you've been, Sunny. I'd never have guessed that you had this in you."

Sunny looked hurt only briefly; then she attacked, "Don't be so high and mighty. It's time I looked after myself. What has goodness, niceness gotten me? A faithless, murdering husband and a murdered lover. Niceness. You, David, that's not what you respect, anyway. All you respect is a brittle wit. Clever wit."

"Save it, Sunny. You were clever enough when you sent Tim out. Damn it. That man loves you and you played on it. How? How can you hurt Tim?"

"It's time I played by the same rules as the rest of the world. Don't think Tim's so perfect, anyway," Sunny snapped, as incapable of holding back as Vicki now. "And what do you with your cynicism and walls know about love anyway, Vicki?"

"At least now I know after this conversation that there were probably two sides to the problems in your marriage. Suddenly I'm not so surprised that you two-timed Bob. I seriously wonder if this affair would work any better than any of the others you hinted at—or your marriage."

Fury and hurt at Sunny's words, and fury at herself for violently losing control, blinded Vicki to all other impressions. Turning on her heel she had swept from the room and was in the kitchen before Sunny's horrified expression could register with her.

Vicki found herself leaning against a counter near the sink, the doorway behind her, to the left. It was a small kitchen for a house of this size, feebly lit by two candles on the counter. There was no kitchen table here. Funny that this should be the only furniture missing from the house. Funny she should actually notice.

That's when the tears started. Vicki rather inelegantly rubbed her nose with the back of her hand and snuffled up. She rummaged a tissue from her skirt pocket and blew her nose. Exhausted, Vicki closed her eyes at the thought of Tim and the others outside, at the remembrance of her words to Sunny. Why did she have such a damn temper? Why was it all so mixed up?

Vicki turned, leaning back against the counter, her hand anxiously squeezing her forehead. The hand dropped to rub the back of her neck, and she looked up at the ceiling then down at the floor. No answers in either place. Maybe a cup of tea would help. Hadn't the kettle been moved to the study with Sunny? Not where she wanted to be.

Why had she lost her temper? Why had Sunny said such nasty things, too? Sure Sunny was upset, horribly shaken, but why attack Vicki? That was what shook Vicki the most, to see her friend turn so vicious. *That couldn't have been Sunny. Damn, this was not the time or place to be alone.*

Vicki fleetingly caught herself hoping that this might all be part of a joke staged by Tim and David. It had to be. The only hitches were the chance appearance by Janos Husaruch and the presence of a definite corpse—touches too elaborate even for those two.

Her thoughts drifted back to Janos Husaruch. It really was amazing to find that someone you liked when you were in the shadows of anonymity really did deserve your admiration. He could easily have been arrogant, but he was warm. She could use some warmth now. Sunny had been right about her cynical shield being a mere front; it couldn't kill genuine emotions, and all this horror had unearthed more than she'd expected. Maybe it was the horror of finding a man dead, maybe it was the inconceivable rift between her and Sunny—she just needed the warmth of the camaraderie that had grown between her and Husaruch in the living room. Vicki mourned the loss of a new ally now.

The hitch was: his warmth toward her was all too good to be true. Why should Janos Husaruch, of all people, be attracted by her writing? He couldn't see into her, could he, just by reading her books? Dared she believe him?

Yet, despite all logic, she trusted him and wished him back safe—and of course Tim and David, too. He made her not want to feel prickly or defensive. He made her want to feel the way she had ages ago, before experience had wised her up. She didn't want to be on guard with him. But *should* she feel this way? Hadn't she misread signs before? What about that summer with David?

That was when Vicki heard the sound. Muffled, cut off. A cry? A creaking board? The wind? Her imagination. What else could it be? Vicki wasn't even sure she'd heard a sound. Ignore it. This was an old house sitting in the middle of a malicious storm. Groans were only to be expected. Or had that been Sunny?

What to do? She had to look. Of course it was nothing; she had nothing to lose by looking. And anyway, she had locked the door after the men left. Right? Of course, she had. She'd promised she would. She just couldn't picture herself doing it.

Still, this had been a night for the unlikely—and Sunny was alone now. That's when Vicki halted her step forward. She was alone, too—and certainly no Gary Cooper. She hated herself for the hesitation. But she couldn't be stupid, either. Swiftly, she scrambled about the kitchen, looking for some form of protection. Nothing, not even a fork. Vicki was ready to start cursing the former tenants for taking the silverware with them when she remembered there might still be a poker left by the living-room fireplace.

As she dashed for the living room, Vicki caught herself snatching again at the practical possibility of this being the fault of her imagination. After all, hadn't more than enough gone wrong tonight already? What was a stupid question to ask tonight!

Miraculously not slamming into anything in the semi-darkness, Vicki found one poker left. Would that Janos had left that knife on the table. Right! Anyone with a brain in his head would have left a knife lying around by itself in this house tonight!

Anyway, the poker was what she wanted. A long-range weapon. No close quarters scuffling knife fighting for her. Vicki turned back toward the study and felt an Arctic rush inside. Had she closed the doors behind her when she'd stormed out? Just as with locking the front door, she couldn't remember. The fire burning behind her made everything look murky. Why couldn't she remember? Until this moment, she'd never realized how accurate a description "clammy" was for fear. She hefted the poker determinedly and crossed the foyer.

Vicki found herself in front of the closed double doors. It was silent in there. Of course it was silent; a murderer certainly wouldn't be advertising his presence. Then again, she really might have pulled the doors closed behind her and forgotten in her fury. Or maybe Sunny had gotten up and closed them herself. The front door was closed, should she check to see if it was locked? *Maybe I've been writing too many mysteries.*

Then again, if David and Tim entered now and saw her hefting this poker she'd have to grant that they'd won their bet. She really hated dark and stormy nights. Well, perhaps if Sunny saw her with the weapon, she'd be the first to apologize. Vicki smiled and decided it was time both she and Sunny agreed to bury the hatch...forgive and forget.

"Sunny?"

No answer. Probably asleep. Pushing open the left of the double doors, Vicki was surprised to see the fire banked down. Perhaps Sunny had found the heat excessive. Whatever, Vicki could see Sunny resting peacefully on the couch, facing away from her. Vicki smiled, embarrassed to have entered the room with a deadly poker, but also amused at her motherly instincts as she put down her weapon and went to pull up the blanket tangled at Sunny's feet.

Vicki started to pull up the blanket, when she noticed Sunny slept too peacefully, the result of vicious weals on her neck from a scarf cruelly knotted, the woman's face horribly twisted from her death throes. Repulsed, almost stupefied, Vicki stepped back into a sharp crack on the head that reduced her horror to swirling, spiraling blackness.

Chapter Five

Everything was so darkly vague, like trying to peer through gauze into a murky swamp. Vicki wasn't even sure if her eyes were open. Well, maybe they were half open. And her head. What did she feel? An ache? She was too dazed to feel pain. She was hazily aware that she was propped up.

Someone was with her. Terror flashed and was gone before she could react or understand. She thought her eyes opened a little more. There seemed to be a man; his voice somehow reached her, but she wasn't sure what he said. Was she discerning dark hair surrounding a whitish face?

"Janos?" she tried to say, but her throat was dry, her head was sore. Her words hushed inarticulately. No, the other voice wasn't his. It was different, but the concern was real and, surprisingly, gentle.

The surprise made her blink and open her eyes as she breathed, "David?"

She could focus better and saw David smile with relief. They were in the parlor now.

"I thought you were a lost cause. You were so still when I found you."

"Found? Oh my God!"

David's words made her remember everything, driving Vicki to try and pull herself up. At her sudden movement, Vicki's skull had other ideas. The top of said noggin seemed to rocket somewhere into the stratosphere with Flash Gordon.

"I found her, Vicki; calm down," David urged quietly, firmly holding her back, but somehow sparing her tender skull from having to touch the couch. "There's nothing you can do."

"She's dead?"

Vicki saw David flinch at the guilt and pain that accompanied her question. He moved closer to her and gently insisted, "It's not your fault."

"I left the room," Vicki shot back. "We'd had an argument."

She didn't know if it was the head blow or her anguish, but she started to feel nauseated.

"If you had stayed, would things be different? Sunny still would have been attacked. You could still have been knocked unconscious, or even killed. Would that have improved the situation? And if you're guilty, aren't we all? I and Tim and your friend, Arthur Rubenstein, we left you both alone—and at whose insistence? Sunny's. Now who's ultimately at fault?"

"You're a good lawyer," Vicki conceded, closing her eyes, though not entirely letting herself off the hook. *How had this happened? Another death, this time a friend.*

"I'm going to make a compress for your head. I have a clean handkerchief with me. You never know; there might be some towels in the kitchen. Do you mind being left alone, briefly?"

Vicki clenched her hands in her lap. She decided not to risk shaking her head, instead just replying, "No. Go ahead."

"Fine. I'll be right back," David assured her, rising.

But Vicki stopped him before he reached the door, "David, how long was I unconscious?"

David shrugged, answering, "I can't say, Vicki. You were out when I came in a few minutes ago. I just brought you in here."

"But, David, where are the others? Is something else wrong that you haven't told me?"

"Take it easy, kiddo," David calmed her, walking back to Vicki through the murky firelight. "Nothing melodramatic. Your friend the mad Russian and I got separated. You can't see anything out there. I ended up circling back and saw the front door was open. I rushed in to check if anything was wrong."

"I guess you weren't disappointed," Vicki bitterly admitted, hiding her gaze in her lap. "It's my fault. I think I forgot to lock the door when Sunny called me right after you left. If I'd remembered..."

"Damn it, Vicki, stop!"

David surprised her by his swift stride across the room. He knelt by her and riveted her with his eyes: "You can't blame yourself. Nothing here is your fault. You can't control everything. You can't solve every problem personally. Sometimes other people foul up. I will not let you take responsibility. All insults and ribbing aside, I care too much about you."

Vicki could only stare at David in surprise, his blue eyes fired by the intensity of his feeling. She let him hold her hand tightly, remembering, fleetingly, a summer night long ago.

But neither had time to lapse any further into sentimentality, because Janos Husaruch and Timothy West pushed through the front door, the latter supported by the former.

"Oh, David, look," Vicki breathed, briefly distracting her glance from the storm-bedraggled entrants. Aching for the latest casualty, she finished, pityingly, "Tim."

Janos Husaruch hesitated with his burden, not quite expecting to see David and Vicki in the parlor rather than with Sunny in the study.

"In here," David directed, cutting through the confusion.

"I'll get off the couch; he can rest here," Vicki offered, immediately regretting her decision halfway to her feet.

David eased her back to the couch, as he heard Tim say weakly, "I'm all right. Just help me to the chair. I only need a moment to rest."

Helping Tim into the room, Janos explained, "I found him on the ground, not far from the building, on the side by the study."

As Tim was helped into the chair to the couch's left, Vicki saw his face was battered and bruised, his hands scratched. David moved to his friend's side, regarding him reflectively.

"Tim, what happened?" Vicki questioned, now steady enough to lean forward to see him better.

"I don't know," Tim answered, somewhat dazed. "I think a tree branch might have caught me. I don't remember much."

"Find him under a branch?" David queried of Janos.

"No. Why do you have to ask? He's your friend. Do you think he'd knock himself out?" Janos countered, annoyed with David.

David glanced significantly at Vicki, and she was not happy with what she suspected was on his mind.

Janos did not miss the exchange and questioned, "What's going on? What aren't you telling us? And what happened to Miss Westlake?"

"Do I look that awful?" Vicki managed, trying to forestall the revelation of Sunny's death, particularly in front of Tim.

Janos ignored her words and knelt in front of her, concern shaping his features when he asked, "What happened?"

Out of respect for an equal, she couldn't back down from those dark eyes. And there was sensitivity there, too.

Vicki started to speak, but David cut in, "I think she was bashed by the same person who knocked out Tim, probably when he was escaping."

Vicki's and Janos's eyes lingered only a moment before both sharply turned to David. Janos rose, demanding, "Escaping? From what? What are you keeping from us, Mr. Morrow?"

Vicki tilted her head curiously. She could have sworn she'd seen a trace of jealousy in David's tone, but before she could consider further, Tim demanded: "What about Sunny?"

Tim's voice drew down absolute stillness. Vicki and David couldn't even look at each other, never mind answer their friend. Janos Husaruch picked up on their anxiety if not the exact reason, and his eyes questioned Vicki. She couldn't face him and glanced away, though.

"Damn."

Again the word belonged to Tim as he launched himself from the chair and proceeded determinedly, if unsteadily, to the study.

The others followed, Vicki helped to her feet by a swiftly solicitous David. When they found Tim in the next room, his reaction surprised them. No hysterics, no anger. He'd just sunk into a chair across from Sunny not far from the door. His chin rested in one hand. He stared at Sunny. He said nothing.

They all hesitated, suspended by the gruesome sight of one friend and the emotional bankruptcy of the other. It was Vicki who made her way over to Tim, took one hand, and said quietly, sincerely, "I'm sorry, Tim. I know how much you cared about Sunny. We all loved her, but she's always been special to you. I wish I could bring her back. If there's anything I can say or—"

"Why weren't you with her?"

Vicki flinched, lowering her eyes under the relentlessness of her friend's accusing gaze, now so cold.

"I, I..."

"Why were you in the parlor with David while she was alone in the study? Why did you leave her?"

75

Guilt from that final argument lacerated Vicki and she swiftly got to her feet, backing away, all the while Tim's eyes and words following her like inescapable poisoned arrows.

"What difference does it make where she was?" David jumped in, stepping forward, protectively placing hands on Vicki's shoulders. "Maybe Vicki was thirsty, maybe she had to 'use the facilities'. For Christ's sake, she's only human. Would you have been happier if she'd been around to be murdered as well?"

"Morrow's observation is morbid," agreed Janos Husaruch, with a skeptical glance at David, "but accurate. As it is, Miss Westlake appears to have a nasty lump on her head. It looks as if the murderer and she met, albeit briefly."

"Is that true, Vicki? Did you see anything?" anxiously tumbled from Tim.

Standing between David and Janos, Vicki answered, "I'm not much help, Tim. I came back to the study, saw the doors closed, couldn't remember if I'd closed them myself, picked up a poker for protection, went in...saw Sunny—and then I guess someone hit me, knocked me out from behind."

"Is that all? You didn't see who did it? How he got in?"

"Who did it?" David flared. "We know it must have been Bob. Anyway, how can you say 'is that all' to Vicki? Someone knocked her out cold. Would you be more satisfied if there were a little gray matter on the floor?"

Seeing Vicki wince at that crack, Janos warned, "Just stick to the facts, Morrow. Hasn't this woman been through enough?"

"Certainly, and I'm trying to save her from going through any more. Who are you, anyway, to insinuate yourself as her champion? I've known her since she became an expert in snowball trajectory over twenty years ago. Maybe you're letting your reputation as a savior of the persecuted go to your head..."

Vicki wasn't sure of Janos's comeback, probably something provocative and witty, because David was busy lancing back. She just couldn't stand the bickering, not with this head, not with this guilt; so she edged away from the men. Unfortunately, where she now stood afforded much less peace of mind. Nothing blocked sight of Sunny's body still stretched on the couch, the scarf knotted lethally around her neck. Why hadn't David removed it, given the woman some dignity, at least now? Oh, of course, evidence. The police investigation. No one can afford to destroy evidence. Besides, he might have been too concerned with the living: her.

That was odd. Vicki looked closely at the knot as if she'd never seen it before, the familiarity of the way it was tied. Something clicked into place inside her, something she didn't like.

"David, Mr. Husaruch," she interrupted. "Come over here, quickly. Something's not right."

"What?" spoken in unison by the two.

"The knot, look at the knot. It isn't right."

"What do you mean?" questioned Janos.

"It's around the neck of one of my best friends," David noted dryly. "That's not right."

Vicki resisted the urge to thump David, persisting, "It's a left-handed knot."

"What?" At last David was befuddled.

Vicki elaborated. "My brother is a leftie. That's the way Ben used to tie his knots when he wasn't at school and the nuns weren't trying to make him into a rightie. The knot of a right-handed person looks slightly different."

"So?" David questioned.

"So, Sunny had told me that Bob is right-handed."

David blinked.

"Could he have disguised his knot?" Janos questioned.

"Not Bob. He isn't that clever," David asserted.

"If anything," Vicki continued, "Bob wouldn't have had the time to fake a left-handed knot. Sunny wouldn't just sit there, tapping her fingers, waiting to be strangled. Believe me, from the way Ben used to complain, I can tell you it's almost impossible at first to use the 'wrong' hand."

"Then if this Bob isn't the murderer," began Janos carefully, "who is?"

Vicki started to speak, but couldn't, chilled by the thought that by eliminating Bob as a suspect she had narrowed the field down to—the people in this room?

"Fine amateur detective," burst out Tim bitterly. "You've narrowed the field down to us. And since I'm left-handed—and look, scratches on my hands, maybe from a struggle?—I must be guilty. Or maybe I got them pushing through some bushes when we were outside."

"At least I'm off the hook," chirped David, trying to lighten the situation, "I'm right-handed. Ever seen me using my left hand?"

Tim glared at David. David shrugged at his failure.

However, it was Janos's psychology that worked best.

"I guess we're guilty together, Mr. West. I'm left-handed as well. Of course, you, I, and the rest of us are innocent for the same reason: not one of us has a motive to kill either your friend or her lover. I don't even know the woman, and the four of you were friends. Where's the motivation for murder? What I suspect is that some person, unbalanced for whatever reason, stumbled onto the man upstairs and killed him, was afraid to venture too far in the storm, came back here and attacked Sunny and Vicki. Perhaps he has some sort of delusions that made him see this place as his home and anyone who entered as dangerous invaders. I've seen people crack before and be swallowed up by their paranoia. They become totally convinced of their delusion. They can't recognize reality."

"Tim," Vicki began reflectively, "what about the people who lived here before? Didn't you tell me that there was someone left alive? Could this person feel cheated?"

"I don't know exactly. I did tell you about the distant niece, but I don't know if she looked at selling the place as a loss or a godsend," Tim answered. "Sunny handled this house. I'd have to go over the records."

"Well, if she lost the house over the last few years, during the Depression, think what it might have done to her?" Vicki reflected. "Oh, I've seen how frightened and bitter and hopeless people have become since the crash. You know how hard it was on my parents. People have been especially edgy lately, with the war in Europe and Asia and the market acting funny again. You people were lucky, you had work, you just don't know."

"But part of my job was to see people lose their homes, their lives," Tim quietly disagreed. "I understand. It's just the ultimate horror that Sunny should die from this."

"I think, Mr. West," observed Janos, "you could use a rest."

"And a compress for that ugly welt across your forehead," Vicki agreed.

"Looks like it's my turn to be compassionate," added David. "You look whiter than the sails on some of the craft I've rowed past on the Charles, Tim, my friend. I'm going to take you into the parlor where you can rest on the couch." He turned to Vicki, "And while you're getting a compress for him, take care of yourself."

Vicki watched David help Tim from the room, then turned back to Janos and said sincerely, "Thank you."

"For what?"

"For restoring some sanity. I never thought that I'd be relieved to know that I was being stalked by an unknown homicidal maniac."

"It's much more comforting to know that most maniacs are strangers, not your friends," he quipped.

Vicki smiled slightly, and though not really wanting to go, started to move past Janos to leave the room.

"Wait, Vicki." His hands, lightly placed on her arm and shoulder, arrested her as much as his words. "Are *you* all right?"

"I'm likely going to have a whale of a headache tomorrow, but I don't think there's anything serious," she assured him, glad of the chance to stay a moment longer.

"A concussion can sneak up on you."

"Thanks for cheering me up."

"I only speak from experience. I once caught my head on a piano lid, don't ask how, and hours later, in the midst of a concert, I sprawled over the keys in what reviewers considered one of the most dramatic conclusions to Rachmaninoff on record."

"Melodramatic," Vicki smiled. She liked the way those amber-brown eyes of his smiled into hers. For the first time she welcomed the way they seemed to melt through her defenses. Only at this moment did she truly realize how much she could use a haven from this nightmare—even in a stranger.

"Thank you," she said quietly, "again, for bringing back the sanity. You were kind to Timothy. He needed it. I think you have a good heart."

"Then we have something in common."

She started to protest, but he insisted, "I've meant what I've said to you tonight, Vicki. I think there's something special in you. Don't get me wrong, please. I'm not trying to snow you. I've seen too much over the past few years to mince words or play games."

Vicki hesitated. She really felt as if she could believe him. That he was on the square. So much had happened tonight, too much for her cynicism to save her from. She found herself admitting, "Fate certainly could have found more felicitous circumstances to bring two people together."

This time Vicki's tone was not bitter, and they started to smile until Janos saw the pain in her features as she recognized at whose excuse she had made her joke. He held her close as she started to cry, releasing much of the anguish and turmoil tormenting her this night. He knew very well the necessity of crying, after losing Barbara, fleeing Europe. And to him, her clasp felt good, her body warm, and her chestnut hair soft against his face—a comfort that now forced him to recognize how this night's events had torn him, too.

And Vicki let herself go. Let go of the bitterness of the night, of so many years past, and of the horrors of the world around them. She accepted and was comforted by the warmth he offered her. Death wasn't just in Europe, Asia; it was here in her personal world tonight. Coldness and cynicism were no protection. They had to search out security, perhaps by helping each other?

When Janos offered his handkerchief so she could blot her tears and give her nose a good blow, she gratefully accepted. Still letting him hold her, Vicki finally faced him to wryly note, "Strong arms."

"Necessary for power and precision in playing," he smiled. But they didn't laugh; instead they surrendered to the warmth filling the voids that had been inside them and kissed. Anxiously but still gently, warmly. To Vicki it was release, as if at last she could admit her hatred of those self-erected barriers of the soul by pulling them down—no, more accurately, by letting him flow through with that gentle, sweet persuasiveness. Lord, it felt so good to brush against his cheek, to touch his hair, to sweetly seek out each other's lips again and forget everything but their need for each other's kindness, passion, warmth. But there was so much to forget.

And then they both pulled abruptly away from each other, both blinking awkwardly at that sweet but crazy lapse.

Husaruch started, "I'm sorry. You must understand, I don't usually..."

Vicki raised her hand to silence him, able only to say, "We can't...I don't know what came over me, us.... It's far from the right, time, place, isn't it?"

And on that ragged understatement, Vicki strode swiftly from the room, down the shadowy hallway toward the kitchen. But not before she had seen Janos Husaruch's eyes. Despite his words, those eyes told her that he hadn't been any sorrier than she for that moment of escape they'd given each other. Such was Vicki's turmoil that she was halfway down the corridor before she realized that she was moving headlong down a *dark* corridor, into the kitchen, alone—with a twice-lucky homicidal maniac somewhere around.

Vicki halted and looked behind her. Janos was nowhere in sight, but David stood in the doorway of the parlor, his features obscured in the house's gloom. *How much had he seen from the open doorway?*

"Vicki, wait," he called quietly. "I'll go with you."

Normally, Vicki wouldn't have relished finding out just what David had seen of her and Janos Husaruch; however, "normally" was the last adverb any one could use for this evening. Anyway, to be honest, she anticipated stepping into an isolated room, alone, with about as much joy as the Polish greeted the Germans in Warsaw. So she waited.

As David approached, Vicki took the initiative and questioned, "How is Tim?"

"Resting. There's no way I can say Sunny's death didn't knock him for a loop, but he's quiet now, at any rate. What I worry about is that blow from the branch. I'm a lawyer, not a doctor, Vicki. I don't know beans about a concussion or a fracture."

"I'd think a fracture would leave him something less than ambulatory, David. He probably just had the wind knocked out of him. Although, you ought to recall he isn't the only one who was cracked on the head tonight."

They had entered the kitchen.

"I know. That's why I was, shall we say, somewhat 'alarmed' by that little performance by you and Paderewski in the study."

Vicki halted, furious, not quite trusting herself to speak.

"I couldn't help but notice," David quietly defended himself against her gorgon stare.

Turning abruptly away to search a nearby cabinet draw for something to use as a fresh compress, Vicki retorted cooly, "You wouldn't have seen anything if you hadn't been spying."

David grasped Vicki's shoulders and turned her around, her antagonism melting into surprise as she saw his genuine concern.

"Vicki, I care about you. I'm worried."

She glanced down, flustered. *How to react? This wasn't typical David—so open.*

"I can take care of myself," she finally answered, not sure she sounded any more assured than she felt.

"Two murders in the house and you think I'm trying to take away women's suffrage? Vicki, I don't think I can take care of *myself* here."

"But if we stick together, like Janos…"

"'Janos says'? Do you buy his malarkey about some lunatic unhinged by financial difficulties? He's covering up."

"Covering up? What do you mean? David, you don't think one of us could be the murderer? That's insane."

"Is it? Some of us have better motives than a misdirected lunatic would have."

"What? Who? What on earth are you talking about?"

"Vicki, you saw just as clearly as I did how Sunny reacted when you implied this fellow upstairs was her only lover. Embarrassment. Guilt."

Vicki pressed her lips together. Unable to bring herself to add that Sunny had admitted as much to her later, she only managed a tight, "Go on."

"Your friend Janos could have been another man in her life."

"What? David, are you nuts? He never even met her before!"

She didn't like the way his accusation sliced into her heart.

"Really? How do we know for certain? Sunny looked terribly startled to see him."

"Did she, exactly?" Vicki protested, crushing down the vicious imp of doubt David had stirred. "She was probably shocked to see a stranger in her trysting place. After all, most people don't invite concert pianists along on their affairs, even for mood music. I mean, at least she knew us and about this stupid plan for a night in a creepy house. Just not this one, I guess."

82

"Or maybe she was shocked to see a former lover in the same house where her current paramour had been murdered?" David pushed intently. "Don't you remember how swiftly he leaped forward to introduce himself, insisting she didn't know him—a signal for her to keep quiet about him, perhaps?"

"The truth, perhaps?" Vicki countered defiantly. "For God's sake, David. If she did suspect Janos, I think she certainly would have blown the whistle on him."

"She had another suspect, at first, Bob—and now that she's dead she can't voice any further suspicions."

"No! I don't buy this!" Vicki insisted, moving assertively away, stopping at the kitchen door, and staring at the wind-whipped trees through the window. Her reason kicking in, she turned back and argued, "If you blame Janos, why not blame any of us? Why not accuse Tim of being the jilted lover? He's worked with Sunny for years. We all know he's carried a torch for her even longer. Maybe he snuck in, murdered her, then snuck back out and feigned his injury. He is left-handed, and he's always had access to this house."

"That's true," David agreed, though not giving up, "which goes to show that an outsider is less likely to be the murderer."

"Well, why stop there," Vicki insisted quietly, but confidently now, crossing to David. "Maybe *you* are the mystery lover. Or maybe *I* murdered Sunny in a rage. We did have a nasty argument while you boys were out on your hunt. Maybe she'd stolen *my* lover—and then, of course, I hit myself over the back of the head for an alibi. Better yet, my subconscious has replaced the untenable memories of murder with acceptable ones. I guess that makes my sore noggin just psychosomatic. Maybe I've been hiding being a south paw all these years."

"You're not upset about my theory in general," David pointed out. "You're upset about a particular application—to Janos Husaruch."

Vicki blushed before she could reply indignantly, "That is absurd."

Damn his lawyer instincts.

"Vicki," he sighed, "you don't know the man. He's probably a slick artist. How much can you trust a musician? You know people like him play other people like they play their instruments. You're usually so on the ball; how could you let his charm buffalo you?"

"That's a nice load of—stereotyping," Vicki shot back, once again inwardly wincing at the strong possibility that David could be on the money. But she was also pulling together some unexpected truths, herself, that David might not be aware he was giving away.

"You never liked the man from the moment you saw him. Even before you really talked to him or took the time to know him, you were about as warm to him as Roosevelt to the Supreme Court. Where did the analytical lawyer's mind go? When did knee-jerk reactions start?" she probed insightfully.

David tried to joke, "I'd rather be compared to one of the 'nine old men' than to Roosevelt."

Even with his smart talk, David couldn't suppress a squirm at the piercing green eyes that greeted his crack. He considered uncomfortably before blurting out, "All right. I'm jealous, damn it."

Vicki's eyes widened. She stammered, "Of him? Why on earth? You don't even know him?"

"But I know you. What you think of him, seeing you two together, him charming you...."

"What? Why would you care? I don't understand."

"I *care* about *you*."

The words came out with difficulty, but they came clearly, insistently. For once, David's blue eyes weren't laughing.

"Me? Well, yes, as a friend. We've always been friends. But that's not what you mean? Me?" Finally, Vicki protested lamely, "But I'm not even your type."

"My type. What do you know about my type, Vicki? There've been so many women in my life. If any one of them were my type wouldn't I have married her? You, you've always been the one I've admired—tough-minded, acerbic, but someone with a good heart—but you never could see me."

"I, I, it never seemed right. I never felt I could, well, I never felt you were, ah, sincere. I'm sorry, David. I don't mean to insult you, but you've always treated your girlfriends so cavalierly. What could you expect me to think?"

David looked down, licked his lower lip, but faced Vicki to say, "I couldn't be sincere with *them*. They didn't want it, not really. They weren't like you—and I had a reputation to live up to. But you were always so distant; warm and funny, but the barrier was there. Maybe that was why, that summer years back, I backed off when I thought things were getting too—out of my hands."

"So you *did* have feelings for me. I didn't imagine it. But all those years ago; what a waste of time. Why did you waste all that time, David?"

David, uncomfortable at letting his own barriers down, certainly not used to it, shrugged, looked away and tried to explain, "I don't know. I guess I always saw myself as that devil-may-care type like Clark Gable or John Garfield, except there was always that one gal who stood up to him, and it took him a whole movie to figure out she was the one for him. Maybe, I kind of see you as my Rosalind Russell or Anne Sheridan. But the thing is, life isn't a movie. Like those gals, you're a strong woman, Vicki. And like those women, you expect a lot from a guy. I guess, I was, uh, nervous, not comfortable. And you were always so on your guard."

"You don't make intimacy easy, David. You don't always know when to draw the line. You can be irresponsible and, well, insensitive. I'm sorry, David."

He shrugged. "You're right, Vicki. I can't argue with that, but I will tell you that I don't want to see you hurt."

"I'm all right," Vicki assured him gently.

"Not with Janos What's-His-Name here."

Vicki started to flare, but kept her cool. David meant well. She couldn't be cruel to someone who'd opened up like this to her, and maybe she subconsciously suspected that Janos Husaruch was too good to be true. Could she have let down all her defenses, not because he was good and kind, but because the night had been so brutal?

"You see there is terrible truth in my skepticism about Husaruch," David interpreted her silence.

"I see that these are not the sort of circumstances in which to make snap decisions," Vicki asserted calmly.

David studied her carefully. So carefully, Vicki wondered if he saw just how close to the bone his words had cut. He didn't press, though. He only said, "Just consider what I've said, Vicki. Don't make any quick judgments." He hesitated, then, his expression rueful, added, "Now I'm going to say something I should have said a long time ago. If you decide to let go of that fiancé's ghost, think about me."

She stared at David, uncertain how to feel.

He smiled again at her and said, "I don't know why I wasn't threatened like this by Eric. Guess I just knew it would never fly. I guess I just took for granted it wasn't a problem, and I didn't really understand you wouldn't always be there. Besides, I think Natalie was keeping me pretty busy at the time.

"I just don't want to see you get hurt again, Vicki. I don't want to see you eighty-sixed by another Eric. Seeing Tim so miserable, seeing Sunny die, I just realize this is my one and only second chance."

Bewildered, Vicki turned back to the cabinet and pulled out a dish towel. How did she feel about David after all this time? Being in control of her feelings was so vital in this moment of emotional confusion. She wet the cloth and wrung it damp, commenting, "All this soul baring made me forget what I came in here for."

She turned awkwardly back to David, handing him the compress, explaining, "This should take care of Tim."

Vicki was uncomfortable under David's eyes. They were gentle and knowing, and she felt guilty. Had she been too flip? What did she want to say?

David nodded, took the cloth, and asked, "Coming back with me?"

"Sure. In a minute. I need one of these myself. I must have a lovely knot on my head, too." She hoped her words were convincingly light.

"I could wait."

"No. I'm fine. I think I need some time to think—and Tim should have a compress. I'm okay."

David turned up the corner of his mouth as he promised, "I'll be waiting for you."

He left Vicki. Who would have thought she'd ever be glad to be alone in this house tonight? No, that wasn't fair to any of the others, all just as confused as she. Still, none of this added up to her. Granted, she felt relieved, justified even, that she'd been right about David that summer years back. But was David really what she wanted? Only a few years ago she might have been ecstatic, but now...Well, exactly how *did* she feel about David after all this time? She'd been so used to seeing him as her friendly antagonist, but still an antagonist. Was that the type of relationship she wanted? Did she really want a relationship with anyone? And then there was Janos Husaruch. What did he have to offer her? Was he actually offering anything? Was he any more on the square than any other man she'd wasted her time on?

Sighing, Vicki crossed to the window on the heavy wooden back door. Funny, that there should be no curtains. Wouldn't it have been like Sunny to replace them if she'd made this a trysting place for her lover? Sunny liked a home.

Vicki closed her eyes. "Liked" would have to be past tense forever now. God, how could she have lost a friend? *Would* Sunny have been lost if she'd stayed with her?

When she opened her eyes there seemed to be no rain driving through the darkness. When she opened her eyes, fear burned her spine as she perceived in the murky candlelight reflection of the window that she was not alone.

Vicki sharply twisted around. Ready to fight? To flee? But she relaxed, feeling a fool as she recognized Tim's solemn features.

"Sorry I jumped, Tim. Being alone here, well, I just didn't recognize you at first. It's been a long evening."

She'd tried to sound light, but her words fell flat and strained on Tim's serious features, dark eyes burned into a white face.

"Are you okay, Tim?" she asked, concerned for her friend. "Did you get the compress? Did it help?"

"I need to talk to you," Tim began.

Vicki hesitated. He was so serious. Something was wrong.

"Certainly," she answered slowly, stepping toward him. "Tim, are you sure you're all right?"

"It's important we talk," Tim insisted, his voice just too restrained.

For a moment, Vicki dreaded *he* would confess an undying love for her; it seemed the latest vogue tonight. Hesitantly, she urged, "Go on."

"It's about Sunny."

Vicki began to chew her lip. She'd heard Tim tense, shaky, but never with this quiet, even white-lipped, control.

"I want to know. Did she tell you about who her other lover was?"

"Other lover?" Vicki cringed at the fake casualness of her response. He knew she was lying, but how did he know there had been someone else? She didn't think he'd been in the room when Sunny had reacted strangely to her words, or had Sunny said something she hadn't heard? Could Tim have even intercepted a note or a phone call? She knew she was taking too long to answer. He'd be suspicious that her delay meant she was trying to figure out how much to hide from him.

"She wouldn't have had anyone else. Not Sunny," Vicki corrected him, she so hoped gently *and* convincingly. Bad enough he'd lost Sunny without his believing that she'd passed him over for three other men. *Sunny, if you'd chosen Tim from the start, you'd be alive now.*

Tim's lower jaw shifted, tensed. His dark eyes had never appeared, so, well, yes, relentless. He finally stated, eyes locking hers, "I don't want any lies. I want the truth."

"Why should I lie?"

He folded his arms and probed, "Why *should* you?"

"I think I've heard that question before," Vicki returned, unable to restrain her asperity. She didn't like being needled by someone she was trying to protect.

"From our chat earlier this evening, you sounded pretty thick with Sunny, Vicki. I think you're trying to protect someone."

"I'm trying to protect you."

Tim grasped her so swiftly, so sharply, that Vicki barely had time to feel his fingers bruise her arms. He demanded, "What do you mean by that? What did she say to you? What are you covering up?"

"Tim," Vicki struggled, too shocked to answer him clearly, "What are you talking about? I don't understand."

His grip was strong. She tried to fight the panic that Tim's uncharacteristic actions fired in her. As his grip tightened, Vicki could only squirm like an animal caught in a jagged trap. Devastatingly, Tim did not seem concerned with her answers, only with flaying her with his questions-turned-accusations.

"You're not leveling with me. You're keeping things from me. You and David were laughing at me. Did you make Sunny laugh at me, too? I loved her, only her—and she's dead. You took her away."

"Tim, please, let me go. We never laughed at you. You've got it all wrong."

Fighting against her panic, attempting to reason with her old friend, Vicki tried to convince herself not to see Tim's anger as directed at her—but he seemed lost to his fury. He shoved her back against the cupboards and accused, "She'd be alive if you'd stayed there—if it wasn't your fault in other ways. You made me lose her. I've lost her too many times. It should have worked. She should be with me. You made me think we could be together, married, and then all this came out. Damn you, Vicki!"

Vicki Westlake snapped. Timothy's damnation coming so close to her face, his hands moving up her shoulders, Vicki's self-preservation instincts took over and she channeled her fear and anger into one hell of a shove that sent an unprepared Tim hurling backwards.

Hesitating only long enough to see her former captor stagger, Vicki bolted toward the door leading back to the main body of the house. A door all the way across the kitchen. Halfway across what seemed like a tiled eternity, Vicki heard Tim's heavy step behind her. He'd recovered *that* fast? Her legs suddenly seemed rubbery, her vision blurred. *Now* her injury had to catch up with her? *Damn, no!* The murk of the kitchen, her dizziness, made it all a nightmare.

"Janos! David!" she managed to call.

Vicki was almost at the door, and Tim was almost at her. Shoving the door open, Vicki's landed herself into the shadows of the corridor—only a split second before Tim caught her and whirled her violently to face him.

"What the hell is going on?!" demanded David from the hallway.

Vicki and Tim both turned to see David and Janos poised outside the parlor. Tim shoved Vicki away with a frenzied, "No, you're all against me! You don't understand! I bet his car," pointing at Janos, "isn't even that badly stuck. I'm beating it out of here and going for the police. They'll fix you all!"

And he was gone, back through the kitchen.

Vicki stared wild-eyed as Janos and David rushed to her. She only managed a dazed nod when Janos grasped her shoulders to question, "Vicki, are you all right? Did he hurt you?"

"I'll take care of her," David snapped, jerking Vicki away so sharply that she almost bumped into him.

Concerned, he questioned, "Did he frighten you? What happened in there?"

"Of course he frightened her. The woman can't even talk," Janos cut in before Vicki could respond. "Stop harassing her."

David moved Vicki to his right and stepped up to Janos Husaruch, insisting, "Tremendous help you are, Mr. Psychoanalyst. The poor girl's a wreck. We have to find out what he did to her to get her out of shock."

"She'll be in worse shock if you don't stop jerking her about. She's a person, not a marionette. She needs gentleness."

"She needs to face reality. Recall everything. That clears away the shock."

"Why don't the two of you flip a coin over who gets to slap me into sensibility?" Vicki snapped at them.

They both stared at her, David finally saying, "You can talk, Vicki?"

"A feat I've managed since I was about one. Now are you two giants of psychoanalysis finished discussing my case or should I step into the waiting room?"

David and Janos exchanged awkward glances, so Vicki pronounced, "Good, now you'll listen." She hesitated before continuing, "I'm just not sure where to begin. I wish I could sit down and think, but we've got to get Tim. We can't let him run wild. He was crazy in there, questioning me about Sunny and another lover and saying we didn't care. Thinking we were all laughing at him. He's over the edge."

"I know this is going to hurt you to consider, Vicki," Janos began, "but do you think he could be responsible for what happened to your friend Sunny and her paramour, out of jealousy?"

Vicki looked at Janos, pained. Of course she had wondered the same thing, but verbalizing it was just too much. She resisted, shaking her head, in spite of insidiously creeping doubt, "Tim has always been so gentle and patient."

"But at last he snapped?" Janos pressed.

Janos's suggestion hit her like a slap. It took a beat for Vicki to recover and answer, "I can't believe Tim would really hurt anyone. He was intense, even, even rough, with me a moment ago, but I won't believe that he'd really harm me. Anyway, he said he was going for the police."

"Are you certain he wasn't just trying to throw off suspicion?" Janos asked her gently, but probingly. "Are you certain he's the friend you thought he was, especially after the way he roughed you up just now?"

Vicki turned to David, who'd been strangely silent through these charges against their friend and questioned, "David, you don't think Tim could be responsible, do you? He's been one of us since we were kids. Look at me, David. Why aren't you answering me?"

David did, but his eyes were evasive: "Murder doesn't sound like Tim's style—Bob's maybe, though. And of course we're forgetting Husaruch's stranger-with-a-grudge theory. Unless, of course, Janos here thinks you're guilty, hiding being ambidextrous."

"Certainly," Janos replied sarcastically. "Vicki Westlake clearly has the upper body strength to have strangled the gentleman upstairs and hidden him under the bed, but insufficient smarts not to lead us right to the corpse. Of course, knocking herself out by conking herself in the back of the head displays sheer genius—and contortionist abilities that could get her a job in the finest of circuses."

"Sounds to me as if you've given the prospect of my friend Vicki some thought before you decided to defend her," David remarked pointedly. Turning to Vicki, he added, "Nice of this guy to trust you, after he gave you the kind of once-over you'd expect from a homicide detective."

"Where were you, Morrow, when we got separated outside while the women were in here alone?" Janos coolly challenged. "How did you even know to come to this deserted house in the first place?"

Vicki's mouth dropped open, but before she could defend her friend, David seemed to see red and snarled, "Why you...! I didn't even know about this place until Tim brought me here tonight. It was his little secret—apparently Sunny's, too."

"And how do we know that's true?" Janos pressed. "It's not as if we can just ask him, is it?"

David clenched his fists; Vicki's hand fastening on his arm made him pause. As steamed as she was by Janos's insinuations against her friend, she didn't want him hurt. He just didn't know her friends the way she thought she did; the way she *did*. And that pause gave David a chance to think through his anger and pick out a hole in Janos's speculations.

With a smile sharp and knowing, he pointed out, "When Sunny was killed, if I was separated from you, you were separated from me. And isn't it an odd coincidence that you should happen to get into a crash on *this* road on *this* evening? Any accusations you make against me apply equally to you, bud."

"Do you often use the 'I'm rubber, you're glue' argument in court, counselor?" Janos coolly rejoined.

David's blue eyes flared with further sarcasm on the way, but Vicki raised her hands to both of them and commanded, "Enough!"

Startled into silence, both men stared at her and suffered the brunt of her sharp but concerned words, "Stop locking horns and egos. Tim's out there, alone, distraught. If Janos is right in his earlier conjectures—and he likely is because, remember, Sunny, herself, thought it was Bob, Tim's a sitting pigeon—"

"Duck," David corrected.

"Bird of an endangered species," Vicki bit out, "and if we don't get to him before Bob, or whoever, he's going to be extinct. We've got to get out there and bring him back to safety."

"Absolutely not," Janos shook his head.

"What?" Vicki contested.

"You want us to leave our friend out there in danger?" David demanded.

"You two seem to be forgetting that he may *be* the danger," Janos calmly warned. Seeing Vicki's shocked expression, he insisted. "Look, Vicki, one thing I learned when I was on the run from the Nazis was not to take foolish chances. Outside we're vulnerable in the dark and the storm. Even with the lanterns, well, we can see, but it telegraphs our position. We don't know if our nemesis, whoever he is, is armed. If he has a gun—"

"There's no gun," David cut off Janos. To his and Vick's surprised expressions, David explained, "If our murderer had a gun, why would he strangle the guy upstairs? Further, he could have used it any time since we've been here and gotten away. Hey, maybe I can write mysteries better than you, Vick, ole girl."

Vicki scowled at her friend, then turned her attention to Janos to say, "We aren't completely unarmed. You have your knife—"

"He has a *knife!*" David blurted. "And you're nervous about Tim or Bob?"

"I haven't used it, have I?" Janos returned coldly. "*Both* our victims were strangled."

"So, he has a knife and I have...?" David challenged.

"You'll have a poker from the fireplace!" Vicki triumphed. "Just like me when I go out with you."

"Like you?" both men repeated, exchanging annoyed looks.

Janos shook his head, asserting, "Absolutely not. Use your reason."

"What do you mean?" Vicki protested. "I've got to help you with Tim when you find him. I can't just sit and wait, alone, here."

"It kills me to agree with this guy," David countered Vicki, "but he's right. It's too dangerous. I'll feel better knowing you have your own little killer poker, locked up tight behind these thick heavy doors and those inside-the-window shutters. If something dangerous happens, we don't want to be worrying about protecting you as well as saving our own hides. Right, Husaruch?"

Janos gave a long exhale but agreed, "I still think the smartest move is to wait until morning and then the three of us—"

"Tim may not have until morning," Vicki protested. "You didn't leave that family behind in Europe, Janos, even if it would have been smarter, safer. Don't leave my friend behind, please." She turned to David, "And *you* won't forget your friend; I know it. Go ahead. I want you all back safely. I'll get my poker; that should be sufficient protection until you get back."

No one corrected the "until" to "if," but there was a fleeting silence as the thought crossed all their minds.

"All right," Janos relented, but not happily. His steady eyes boring into David's, he ordered, "And this time we stick together. No getting separated like last time. We all know how badly that turned out for the women."

"Agreed," David nodded quietly. Vicki wondered if he was blaming himself for her and Sunny's vulnerability.

"At least we know where to look for your friend," Janos glumly stated. "I don't give him much chance of going anywhere. My car *is* stuck. Maybe

93

he'll calm down and sit out the weather inside it. At least he could lock the car doors against any danger, if he has the sense."

Janos's pause after he finished suggested he didn't have a lot of faith in the sense of his companions. But he continued, a bit reluctantly, "I think those hurricane lamps took too much of a beating when we last went out. When we were first in the parlor, Vicki, didn't you tell me that there are flashlights in the kitchen?"

She nodded.

"All right. I'll go get them and, Morrow, you get our coats together," Janos directed.

David and Vicki were alone for a moment. He smiled slightly before surprising Vicki by taking her hand for an instant to say, "See that you do stay put. I'm running out of friends tonight. I can't afford to lose you, too, smart-talking lady."

Then he kissed her forehead, leaving Vicki blinking with surprise, not only at his action but at the warmth she felt in response. But David didn't stick around to take things any further, striding off the kitchen to join Janos.

What should she be thinking about her feelings now? Vicki gave herself a mental shake. She should be thinking only about these two guys staying safe and finding Tim. The two men returned and joined Vicki at the door, where they shrugged themselves into their trench coats. As David slid his fedora onto his dark head, he and Janos both looked at her with worry, and more? Janos spoke up.

"I locked the back door. Make sure that you close and lock up the shutters in the study. Check the ones in the parlor. Make sure that you lock this one after we go. *No* distractions. Don't let anyone in but the two of us. And you stay put. All right?"

Vicki nodded, pale and concerned.

To lighten the mood, David quipped, "I don't know, Husaruch. Vicki's promising to stay put is an iffy proposition at best. Maybe we need to tie her to a chair."

"You and what battalion of Marines," Vicki shot back, trying to keep up morale.

But Janos wasn't amused. Whether he was uneasy about leaving her alone, about having to go on an iffy search, or both, Vicki wasn't sure. If she hadn't been so concerned for her friend Tim, she would have told them to stay. It was Janos's dark eyes she saw last as he closed the door behind him and David after saying, "Stay safe."

She only nodded.

Her two "protectors" were gone, leaving her alone with the remains of Sunny and the man upstairs. That realization produced a body-wracking shiver. But, not about to let herself fall to pieces, Vicki forced herself to do the practical thing, rushing to flip the lock on the plate beneath the doorknob. Now, nobody would get in without a key. Did Bob have a key that could have let him in before—or had Tim used one of the keys from his office?

After following Janos's directions concerning the Indian shutters, Vicki wandered restlessly back into the foyer. Her eyes fell on the three raincoats hanging on the wall pegs to her left: her own; Sunny's never to be worn again (she squeezed her eyes tight to keep from crying); and Tim's. So determined to get away, Tim had run out without coat or hat: determined from fear or guilt?

Vicki cocked her head to the side, a thought coming to her. She couldn't just sit around and brood here, but maybe Tim's coat could hold a clue. Maybe if she searched the pockets she might find something, anything, that could clear him—or just the opposite. That last possibility made her hesitate.

NO! She couldn't allow herself to fear the truth. That truth could be invaluable to all three men caught out on this miserable night. If she could absolve Tim, they could know for sure that Bob was their enemy; they could band together against him. And if she discovered anything to point the finger at Tim? Her friend? That gave Vicki pause, but not for long. She would warn her other friends so they wouldn't be caught off guard by Tim's either feigning weakness or misdirecting their caution with lies about Bob.

Her hand was in the left pocket of Tim's trench coat. Nothing. Well, a pack of gum. Nothing so dangerous there. Now the right? A little pocket change. That was it. She was relieved? No, because she knew that an expensive men's trench coat like this would have an inner vest pocket. If a person had a secret to keep, *that* would be where to keep it.

Vicki's hand slipped in and she froze. Her fingers had fastened on paper, rough as if crumpled and re-flattened and folded.

It doesn't have *to be anything incriminating.*

But Vicki couldn't bring herself to pull out her discovery. Not at first. Then, as if ripping a Band-Aid off a wound, she jerked the piece out, pain emotional rather than physical.

The quality of the paper was good. Like a woman's notepaper. Vicki had seen that paper before. Had received messages on it before. Nevertheless, she had to unfold the crumpled, partial sheet and look for the signature.

"Sunny."

The note *could* have been something innocuous, except that it had been crumpled as if in anger and ripped, leaving only the bottom part. In a weird clash of reluctance and determination to know, her eyes scanned the words on this quarter of a page:

> Leave me alone! I've made my choice and it's not you! If you
> try to make things hot for me over Jon, I'll find a way to make
> them even hotter for you.
> Sunny

That staggered Vicki. All this time that Tim had been acting as if he had been afraid to let Sunny know how he felt, he'd been pulling the wool over their eyes?! *He'd* been harassing her?! Why hadn't Sunny ever said anything?! The two seemed to be getting along all right now—although there had been that time over a year ago when they'd had the falling out; Tim had said it was over her not leaving Bob after all his mistreatment. When was this written, anyway? Had Tim, sweet Tim, been nursing resentment all this time? Could tonight's whole "prank" have been a front for his plan from the beginning to do in this Jon? And Sunny's death? Planned or a crime of opportunity? After all, Tim had the keys to this house, so like Sunny he could have gotten in any time. Maybe those scratches on his hands that he'd boldly pointed out hadn't come from the thorny shrubbery as he claimed.

She had to warn Janos and David. Yes, they were armed, but who knew what else Tim was hiding. He could have had a weapon stashed in the car or in the woods. Woods he had admitted knowing well from hunting trips. It would have been too messy to try to shoot them all in the house, but now that he was desperate and they were separated, with Janos and David out in the night...well, Lord only knew what he might try. No bloodstains to worry about outside; and those woods were dark and deep.

Vicki threw on her raincoat and trilby, jamming the paper in her pocket. A few minutes later, warily hefting a poker in one hand, she retrieved the flashlight, tucking it under her arm as she unlocked the door. She carefully pulled the door open and noted the rain had stopped—but fog was drifting up from the road. The wind was still nasty. Bad and good news. Maybe she wouldn't see her way as well even with a flashlight, but she might not be seen as easily, either. She'd better hold that flashlight down so its illumination wouldn't easily give her away. Gripping her poker tightly, Vicki stepped out onto the porch. Her gaze swept the forest-encircled clearing that fronted the house.

Nothing. No one. Just the wind roaring like a freight train through the tops of the trees. Without moonlight, those trees seemed a black, overwhelming mass, rising and writhing into the endless pitch that was a starless sky. Vicki strained for sounds. Nothing. No one calling for Tim. No sounds of struggle. Only stillness.

Raising her coat collar and pushing her hair down under it to keep it from blocking her vision in this wind, Vicki looked back at the house. Dark, empty, except for what was left of Sunny and her lover. A trysting place turned mausoleum. No, she couldn't go back in there. She didn't belong. And after those last angry words with Sunny that had broken their friendship and left the other woman vulnerable to murder, Vicki felt an obligation, a debt that could only be paid off if she somehow took part in bringing back the murderer, even if it was Timothy West. Above all, she owed it to Janos and David to warn them about exactly what they were up against. Not one more person would suffer because of her.

Vicki pushed on across the clearing, against the wind. There were Tim's and Sunny's cars shoved off the road, into a tree, bumpers inextricably locked. The door to Tim's car now hung open. Had he stopped to retrieve something from it? Something deadly? She had to push on and warn the two men who would have to confront Tim about his guilt.

Vicki reached the opening in the stone wall that led to the road and stopped. As she recalled from their initial conversation by the fireside, Janos's car should be about a half mile down the road to her right. Ought she cut into the woods so she wouldn't be a sitting duck on the road? No. She didn't know that she *would* be alone in those woods. Even if the sodden leaves disguised her footfalls, they could do the same for Tim. The deepening fog on this muck of a road might actually hide her better, and she could move faster to catch up with the gents she sought to warn. She just wished she could see them. She couldn't even hear them. Well, *would* they be chattering away, top of their lungs, if they were trying to avoid Bob or not spook Tim? After all, *they* hadn't found Sunny's note in Tim's coat pocket.

What Vicki could hear through the fog was the wind still torturing the branches overhead and along the road. It *was* branches making that creak, wasn't it? Not someone stalking her through the gloom? She valiantly fought down the urge to flash her light into the trees to check—and give away her position.

What was that in the road ahead, caught by her flashlight's beam bled out by fog?!

Vicki took a chance and dashed a few feet forward, nearly sliding into the muck, recovering herself at the last minute, splattering her hose and her skirt.

She reached down and retrieved a man's hat. David's hat! She shuddered. The mud was splashed about as if someone had fallen. Been knocked down? But nowhere to be seen were David Morrow or Janos Husaruch! She whirled around, losing her caution long enough to flash light through the trees, trees that hemmed her and fog that enshrouded her. Vicki just managed to check herself before she shouted their names.

That was when the wind suddenly dropped to reveal the sound of a car engine down the road. *Was it help?* If she'd still really suspected Bob, she'd have wondered if he had hidden his car further off and returned to it to make an escape, now that everyone had left the house. A thought snaked insidiously into her brain. Why had Tim had any reason to think Janos wasn't honest about his car being permanently stuck? What did he, could he, know about Janos that she didn't? She'd never actually seen Janos's car stuck. She had only Janos's word. The word of a man she'd only met this evening, yet who still had the charm to pass through her defenses, like—damn, why did she think of the vampires of *Dracula* sifting through cracks of a window as specks of dust wafted on moonbeams? That was crazy! Janos had defended her, just like David. But where *were* Janos and David? Maybe at the car? Maybe they were fixing it or attempting to get it free. Or maybe Tim had finished them off and was trying to free the car to get away? The engine idled on, down the road.

Vicki gnawed her lip. *What to do?* Galloping back in the house and bolting the door seemed the wisest bet. She was beginning to empathize with Britain's Mr. Run-away-and-Hide-from-Reality, Neville Chamberlain. She certainly could have used his ubiquitous umbrella tonight. Still, if a passerby had stopped on the road for some reason, perhaps to sit out the storm, the idling of his car indicated that he'd soon be leaving. She'd lose a vital opportunity to get help if she didn't nab him. That was, of course, if she could recognize in time the difference between a helpful passerby and a murderer.

Well, no one said she had to make a direct approach. Maybe the forest could be her ally at this moment. Vicki obscured her position once more by pointing her flash's downward for illuminating her way, then moved into the ankle-deep carpet of leaves in the forest. As much as she hated soaking her feet in this dampness, Vicki was grateful the leaves were no longer brittle enough to crackle underfoot and give her away. She wanted the upper hand when she reached the car, just in case.

Now she could pick out through the trees the double swath sliced into the night by the headlights. Vicki pivoted to creep toward the road for a clearer view, silently coming up behind the car—until her foot caught a tree root beneath the leaves, jerking her to the ground. Vicki froze.

How much noise had she made? The engine sputtered out. A stall? Or had she frightened the driver off? She hadn't heard the door slam.

Vicki slowly raised herself, tension keeping her from consciously recognizing how much she shivered from the encompassing dankness. The headlights remained on in a silence punctuated only by the wind-punished branches and rain dripping into the leaves and onto Vicki. *Nothing.* This time her shiver was from fear.

Vicki finally stood up, light and poker lost in her fall and forgotten. Quietly, tensely, she approached the road.

With the headlights not angled directly at her, she could see the car. Even in the foggy night, she could perceive that it certainly looked stuck in the mud by the road's side. Maybe two or three people could free it, but one? Vicki sucked in her breath. Was there a form in the car, leaning against the driver's door? It was hard to see. He certainly wasn't sitting up. Maybe someone was hurt? Where *were* David and Janos?

Vicki slowly approached the car, mud squishing beneath her feet. She hesitated. Should she go back and search out her flashlight? Her poker? Did she have time?

Haunted by trepidation, Vicki Westlake froze a few feet from the car. Yes, there was someone slumped between the wheel and the driver's door, face down, away from her, clearly incapacitated and no threat. The thick rain-darkened hair looked familiar.

"David," she breathed, a flame of shock surging through her. Vicki rushed forward, yanked the door open, horrified as a body rolled from the car to land on its back, face up.

For the first time in her life that she could remember, Vicki screamed. But not for David, for Timothy West.

Chapter Six

Numbly, Vicki bent her knees and hesitantly reached out to touch Tim's neck. No pulse. The eyes rolled up, the still form, all confirmed that he was dead. All horrified her, made her ache almost past endurance that this should be, that this could be. In the headlights' backwash greyly illuminating her friend, Vicki recognized it was indeed too late for Timothy West.

Only one sob escaped Vicki as she sank back against the car, coming to sit on the splattered running board. Now the growing blood stain on Tim's white shirt registered with her as well. So that scrap of a letter hadn't been to Tim. It must have been Bob's, and Tim had found it. *Apparently, Bob had found Tim*, Vicki reflected bitterly. Except her eyes wandered to the road where she caught sight of a knife not far from her, apparently dropped in haste. Vicki went colder than all the damp of the evening could evoke as she recognized the ornately carved handle. A heart-wounded gasp escaped her.

Vicki rose, slowly moving forward. She picked up the weapon from the mire and for one anguished moment hated herself bitterly for the urge to hurl it and her suspicions into the darkness of the forest. But she wouldn't be that weak.

For a moment she tried to reassure herself that perhaps Bob had gotten the knife from Janos. *That* was reassuring? He wouldn't have gotten that knife without a deadly struggle. So, there were her prospects: Janos was dead or badly injured—or there was no Bob and somehow Janos had killed her friend!

"Vicki, what the hell are you doing here?"

Vicki whirled in the darkness, recognizing the voice and the night-blurred features of Janos Husaruch stepping out of the fog from the woods across the road, down past the car, flashlight in hand. Instinctively, she held the knife upward, defensively.

He seemed dazed, uneasy, hesitant. Slowly, unsettled by her tense features, Husaruch spoke: "You have my knife. Where did you find it?"

Uncertainly, Vicki began, hoping there was some logical reason for Janos to have lost the knife, "I came out here to warn you about Tim. I found a note in his pocket that seemed to indicate he killed Sunny from jealousy, but *Tim* is dead. Look at that wound. He didn't stab himself. *With your knife.* How did he get your knife? And where is David?"

Janos Husaruch's eyes held hers. Could he see her hand shake? She wanted to run, but he could easily catch her—God, she wished that she were wrong. Trusting him had seemed so natural, but where had trust ever gotten her before? She was horrified at how Sunny's words of bitterness and cynicism seemed so spot on at this moment.

She saw Janos now fully recognize the significance of her holding the knife defensively between them. His eyes pierced her with shock, then anger. She had never felt so alone. So isolated. So friendless. Could this stand-off last until dawn—and even if she were rescued from it, would she ever be rescued from this inner emptiness? God, she was even afraid to entertain the flickering hope that she was wrong about Husaruch. Where *was* David?

Janos's eyes seemed to threaten to engulf her. What was in those eyes? She couldn't take the silence coupled with the doubt-fed, growing hollowness within. Finally, he broke the silence.

"You believe I killed your friends?"

"I found David's hat back there—no David. But you are here alone, and Tim's dead. Where *is* David?"

Janos seemed to consider carefully how to address the suspicion haunting Vicki before admitting, "I only wish I knew. David flashed his light in the woods on our right while I was checking the other side; he shouted something about seeing that Bob in the woods. He started after him too fast and we both went down. I must have lost the knife then. David got up and went after him before I could get up. I guess I'd had the wind knocked out of me. I tried to follow him into the woods, stop him from going off half-cocked, but I guess the accident earlier with the car and this fall finally caught up to me. I think I passed out for a bit. Your Bob must have doubled back, found the knife in the road, and, unfortunately, put it to good use."

His tone, his explanation, were reasonable. They did make sense to Vicki. And she wanted to believe him. He had supported her, been on her side, looked after her back at the house. He had believed in her. Still, she couldn't help hesitating.

Janos repeated, quietly assertive, yet compassionate, "Vicki, do you truly believe that I am a killer?"

Somehow the sanity of his words washed across her anxiety and pain. This man saw that once more she needed a friend to help her deal with finding someone she cared about dead. How could she have believed him a murderer? Had her bitterness warped her that much?

"Janos, why Tim?" she finally said, lowering the knife.

"Why anyone, Vicki?" Janos smiled wanly, reaching for the knife. "After that eternity I spent dodging the Gestapo, no form of brutal insanity surprises me anymore."

"Vicki! Stop! Don't give him that knife!"

Startled, Vicki leaped back from Janos Husaruch as David slipped and skidded down from the woods to her left, brandishing his flashlight like a club. Janos paused, startled himself, then fired a fierce glare at David, lashing out, "Morrow, you're out of your mind. Haven't you put this woman through enough tonight?"

"I'm trying to prevent you from putting her through the receiving end of a homicide," David retorted as he joined them. He said quietly to Vicki, "Let me hold the knife, *his* knife."

"How do you know that *this is* my knife?" Janos countered. "I never showed it to you. Did you ever describe it to him, Vicki?"

At this vital question, Vicki studied David questioningly, uncertainly. She couldn't *remember* describing it. That didn't mean she hadn't, but...she had a bad feeling again. Who else had a knife, anyway? Who else had *this* knife?

David smiled and with biting glibness countered, "Then where *is* your knife, Husaruch? Don't tell me you conveniently lost it when you conveniently bumped into me and knocked me down. Too bad for you that you forgot to retrieve it after killing Tim. And maybe you'd better drop your flashlight before you get any big ideas about using it on us."

David reached out and supportively squeezed Vicki's hand at these words. Vicki, confused, could only glance silently, intensely, from David to Janos as each spoke.

Janos complied reluctantly with Daivd's order, then queried cooly, "Just a minor point, Mr. Morrow. Wouldn't I need a reason for killing your friend, Tim and your other friend, Sunny, not to mention the gentleman Miss Westlake found under the bed? Or am I merely responsible for one homicide? Perhaps Miss Westlake offed the other two people. She was alone with the victims."

"True," David smiled triumphantly, "but Vicki certainly wouldn't fit the bill of the scorned paramour. She wouldn't have an excuse for murdering the man in the house out of jealousy or Sunny because she'd thrown you over for someone else."

"What are you saying, David?" Vicki protested. "You have no proof. Look, it must be Bob who's responsible. I found part of a note in Tim's pocket from Sunny telling someone to stay away from her, or else. Naturally, I thought it belonged to Tim, where I found it and all, but it must have been sent to Bob, and somehow Tim got a hold of it. You said you saw Bob in the woods, so he likely grabbed the knife where it was dropped, as Janos said. We've got to do something. He could be getting away while we're fighting among ourselves."

David's triumphant features saddened as he looked at Vicki. Gently, he clarified, "I *thought* I saw Bob. But I never found anyone. And it was damned convenient of Husaruch here to 'accidentally' knock us both down then also conveniently get woozy.

"Think, Vicki, it's just too much of a 'coincidence' for Husaruch to happen to show up here. Maybe he's the one Sunny told to stay away. How else would he know about Sunny's trysting place if he hadn't 'trysted' here, himself? Maybe Sunny had given him a key for just that purpose, which let him slip in and strangle her while you were in the kitchen. Sunny must have talked about us, which would clue him in on how to manipulate us, especially you and your little crush. Besides, he's an expert grandstander. You didn't see him keeping under wraps his rescuing that family, did you? It would only be too much of a conquest to win you over and then silence you."

"You bastard," Janos snarled and moved on David, only to freeze as David pulled a tidy handgun from his coat pocket and warned, "Hold it right there, chum."

"Where the dickens did that come from?" Vicki demanded, shocked and furious over David's earlier protestations of being unarmed.

"Just a little something I decided to keep up my sleeve for an emergency," David grimly answered. Nodding his head at the other man, David added, "I never trusted this guy, and I figured *you* might be too trusting of him, Vicki, for me to share my secret with you. Looks like I was on the money."

Held at bay, Janos Husaruch's eyes were the only sign of his glowering fury.

"Good," David decided tightly. "It's about time you dropped some of that self-confidence. I don't like people who buffalo my friends, especially just to kill them off."

Janos fastened his eyes on Vicki and asked, "And you, Vicki, you believe him?"

Vicki opened her mouth to speak, but too much bitterness had built up in her over the years to let her easily trust him, and David's words did make sense. Why did so much have to depend on her decision? If she trusted this time and was wrong, the mistake would be fatally irreversible.

She ground her teeth before temporizing, "I'll have to go along with David for now. That way, we can get the police and let them determine what happened tonight."

"If we all survive that long," Janos Husaruch remarked.

Vicki couldn't look at him, bitter with herself for being too cowardly to trust and defend him.

Reading his uncertain comrade perspicaciously, David put his arm around her and squeezed her shoulder, saying, "It's okay, kid. It's a dirty trick, playing on your feelings."

"If Miss Westlake has any feelings," concluded Husaruch, coldly resigned to having lost his ally.

Vicki glanced at him sharply, but not long enough to make eye contact.

"Nix on the sarcasm," David ordered. "Let's head back to the house. We'll tie you up and let the police worry about you."

"Will I make it back to the house?" Husaruch queried coolly. "Wouldn't the evening wrap up much more neatly if I died before the police could talk to me?"

"Just move, Mr. Husaruch," David ordered with mock civility, indicating with his gun the direction of where the road wound back to the house. "If I want humor, I'll tune in to Jack Benny."

Janos Husaruch smiled tightly and started down the fog-swirled road. Squeezing Vicki's shoulder again , David smiled wearily and reassured her, "Almost over, kid."

Vicki could only look at him sadly. She just wanted the night to end. Watching Janos's back as they started after him up the road, she was relieved he hadn't looked at her when he'd moved past. Perhaps it was good to have David to lean on after all. There had been too much disillusionment tonight.

They hadn't proceeded far before distance from the car reduced the illumination from the headlights. If that weren't bad enough, the beam from David's flash began to fade, likely damaged by his earlier fall. Between the weakened light and the fog, neither David nor Vicki perceived that Janos Husaruch was gradually edging closer to the border of the forest. Neither noticed until the captive unexpectedly ducked and plunged into the rather forbidding safety of the woods.

But David wasn't caught entirely flat-footed. He whirled, ready to fire, then instead brought Vicki unexpected relief when he paused as if suddenly remembering something and lowered his gun. Turning back to Vicki, he sheepishly admitted, "It's not really loaded. I wanted to bluff him. I only load it when I go to target practice, which was yesterday. Now you know the full reason I never mentioned I had the gun tonight—I didn't want anyone to get too brave, thinking we had more protection than we did."

"It's okay, David. No harm done," Vicki answered, peering at the woods but only seeing the fog. She couldn't quite look at her friend, not for his failure to hold his prisoner but for her own weakness. For only David's lowering the gun had kept her from shoving him to save Janos from being hit.

"I imagine you see me as something of a coward, at best a clown," David allowed, giving his ailing flashlight a shake.

Her sympathy caught, Vicki turned back to her companion and took the over flashlight, assuring him, "No, don't be foolish, David. It's not our job to play G-Men. You did your best. We're both still alive. What more can matter? Let's just go back to the house. He thinks you have a loaded gun. He'll be afraid to bother us there."

"We'll be letting a murderer escape," David seemed to be accusing himself. "Look what happened to our friends, to you."

Turning back to the forest, feeling the walls starting to close in, Vicki concluded resignedly, "There's no place left for him to go."

"That's his problem, not yours, Vicki," David gently corrected, taking her hand. He continued, "This hand is cold. I'd better get you back to a warm fire." He paused to study her wavering expression and urged her, "*We're* among the living."

Vicki smiled weakly, not quite sure whether she might mean her reply, "I guess you're right, David. I'd just like to get away from all this."

"You and I both," David agreed, wrapping an arm around his friend, starting to lead her off, only to step into a muddy rut that sent him sprawling, almost taking Vicki with him!

Recovering herself, Vick witnessed the impeccable David Morrow on his stomach, mud-splattered, and more than a touch steamed. How could she help laughing, "Taking the Elizabeth Arden treatment, David? That's twice in one night!"

David sat up, eyed her irritably, and commented, "As much as I enjoy cheering you up, Vicki, I'd prefer to do it in a way that doesn't raise my dry cleaning bills."

"Sorry," Vicki giggled, more releasing tension than being amused. David shot her one last evil look, then endeavored to retrieve his gun. Vicki aided him with the flashlight's illumination, barely repressing her humor—until she saw David find his gun and pick it up with his left hand, seem to catch himself, then switch the weapon hastily to his right, a little too hastily.

Vicki looked away, she hoped casually. More than the raw cold of the night sliced into her as for once tonight her memory of past conversations was all too clear.

"Vicki?"

Had he seen her reaction? *Recover yourself.* Vicki hoped she didn't turn back to David too quickly. Would her expression or her eyes, give her away?

"You're upset?" he persisted, concerned.

"After what I've been through, should I be nonchalant? Not many people have the luck to find three murdered people in one night," she half-lied, she hoped plausibly. Could she bluff until morning?

"Three strikes and you're out?" David gibed.

"Huh, yes," Vicki laughed nervously, trying not to resent that David's humor had come at the expense of her friends. Quickly Vicki insisted, "Please, let's get back to the house."

David regarded Vicki calmly, then smiled as he said gently, "I think you need to be held, Vicki."

"Oh."

"You don't need to sound so doomed," David teased. "I should never have waited for circumstances like these to make you need it."

Vicki felt melodramatic and foolish when David suddenly wrapped his arms around her and pressed her close. There was warmth in David's embrace. Of course this night, this hideous night, had addled her brain, cast dark shadows over her thinking, and distorted her recollections and perceptions. She hugged herself close to David, dropping the flashlight, and breathed, "Damn, David, I just want it to be over."

"It will be, Vicki," David promised her quietly as he pressed her body closer with the arm holding his gun, just before his left hand jerked her head back by the hair so sharply she shrieked.

"Did my slip of the hand tip you off, Vicki?" he questioned amiably.

"I, I don't understand," she desperately lied.

David smiled charmingly, despite bringing the gun up to Vicki's head with his right hand, and explained, "Before you get any foolish ideas that might prompt me to do something violent before I get the answers I want, let me warn you, Vicki, I lied about the gun not being loaded. I just wanted to quell any questions you might have over the sudden appearance of my gun. Besides, it would be harder to paint Husaruch an aggressor if the bullet was in his *back* not his front. I'm afraid pulling the gun was an act of desperation, something new, unfortunately, I've had to get used to tonight."

He seemed distracted by this admission.

"And how do I know that you aren't lying now, about the gun actually being loaded?" Vicki pressed, trying to take advantage of his distraction without getting herself killed.

David recovered himself, smiled ironically, and queried, "Do you really want to take the chance of finding out the hard way?"

Vicki might play a long shot, but not a horse with only three legs.

David continued, "Good, I see by your expression you're going to be a smart girl. That's fine. So now that we're past pretenses, Vicki, perhaps you'll satisfy my intellectual curiosity. You know I hate loose ends. Are people really so perceptive? I saw your reaction when I picked up the gun with my left hand. Just my being ambidextrous tipped you off?"

Vicki wet her lips and answered calmly, her mind racing to determine a way to get enough leverage to throw her captor, "You lied about being ambidextrous, David. Why lie in front of friends? How could you even think your friends would suspect you, unless you had something pretty bad to hide?"

"That doesn't seem enough to me, Vicki. What other mistake did I make?"

"How about," Vicki began, "if I tell you, you'll let me go?"

"How about if you tell me, I'll kill you quickly—not too painfully."

"What are friends for?" Vicki remarked acidly. "How fortunate for me that I'm the woman for whom you've been carrying a torch."

"There's a difference between carrying a torch and being consumed by it, I'm afraid," David quipped, but wisps of tension seeped through his wit.

"Since I'm not terribly lucky in love, how about we cut cards for my life?"

"How about if you tell me what I want to know, Vicki?"

"Damn it, David. We've been friends for years. How could you do this? Why?"

"Why?" David smiled, more than a little anxiety straining his voice as he explained how the great David Morrow had painted himself into a corner, "Why not survival? I lied about seeing Bob, of course and knocked Husaruch down when I faked a fall. He lost the knife then, and I seized the opportunity to grab it while he was stunned. So then I was able to catch Tim alone before your musician friend could interfere. I calmed Tim down and found out he was going to check Sunny's office for the identity of her other lover. See if she'd kept any kind of records about her rendezvous here with him. I didn't know what Sunny had on me, not for sure. She'd threatened me when we broke up, saying she had evidence to make things bad for me if I didn't stay away—"

"*You* were the lover," Vicki accused. "You slipped that note into Tim's pocket from Sunny—but it was originally to you. You wanted to frame poor Tim."

"Don't look so surprised, Vicki. There's a great deal more to life than what dwells inside that fence you put around your feelings. Anyway, I couldn't take the chance Tim would find something, or that he'd find out that I'd taken the call from the man who was to pretend to be dead or the one from Sunny's lover—so when I caught up to Tim here, I pretended to agree he could get this car out. When he started it, I used the knife Mr. Husaruch had helpfully lost back on the road. I knew if I took it I could use it and plant it to incriminate him. I don't like the thought of Husaruch having you."

"Like you didn't like the idea of someone else having Sunny?" Vicki accused bitterly, the puzzle fitting together.

"She had a hell of a nerve dropping me. So when I found out about this new one, I decided to take care of things myself. I wasn't sure how— funny that *I* should ever go off half-cocked—I guess I just couldn't stand the thought of anyone beating me out. You know how I hate to lose. It seemed that even without thinking about it, I could easily outmaneuver people like them. Break them up. I have to admit I didn't really want Sunny anymore; but I wasn't about to be the rejected one. That's not the way it happens with me."

"Don't you think a double murder is slightly overdoing things?" Vicki queried cooly.

Vicki allowed herself a flicker of hope as David lowered the gun, for once seeming genuinely at a loss as he explained, "It didn't start that way. Everything just seemed to fall into place. Opportunity leaped out at me— then, it all went...haywire...people, events didn't fall into the places I'd assigned them."

"What places, David?"

"It all started when I dropped in on Tim today; both he and Sunny were out."

"Where was June?" Vicki pressed, desperately trying to stretch out her time.

David seemed unable to recognize her ploy, fascinated by his own genius, "The secretary went on break just as I came in and didn't come back until much later. That's how I intercepted the first phone call."

"Phone call?"

"It was a man, for Sunny," David answered, growing increasingly delighted with his own cleverness. "He seemed a bit nervous about talking to me. How could he ever have guessed whom he had on the line? He asked to move up an appointment he had to look at this house, using the same code phrasing we used to use. Sunny was such a fool. How could that woman lack the sense, let alone good taste, to schedule a rendezvous with him in the same place she'd met me? The place I still had a key to. I didn't expose my hand, though; I pretended to take his message, knowing I could use this information to break them up. Maybe a message to Bob?"

"So you killed them both for being tacky?"

"That's the funny part, Vicki. I never intended to kill anyone. The fates just seemed to guide me. Shortly after, another call came through. The fellow whom Tim had hired to play dead for you wanted some additional instructions."

"And you're so good at drawing together facts for a plan of attack. Just like building a case for the courtroom," Vicki drew him on.

"I immediately saw this as my opportunity to strike at Sunny and her lover, myself."

"How could you let this opportunity slip by?"

"Exactly," he concurred, flattered. "As usual, I was Destiny's fair-haired boy. I told the man that I was Tim and I didn't appreciate anyone using my business for practical jokes. If this man ever contacted me again, he'd end up in jail. Needless to say, after that threat, I wouldn't have to worry about some stranger revealing my rearrangements."

"Let me guess the next step. You decided to go out to the house and see this new 'beau' of Sunny's for yourself, but things got a little out of hand?" Vicki suggested.

David frowned at the subtle criticism, correcting her, "Not precisely. I was in seventh heaven on the drive out. There were so many ways I could break them up. Should I play on his jealousy by revealing that he wasn't Sunny's first lover? Should I play the innocent, betrayed lover trying to save him from the same fate? Should I pretend to still love her and try to frighten him off? The possibilities seemed limitless for a man of my intellect. They'd be playthings."

However, David seemed to downshift as he mentally replayed the afternoon. He hesitated, almost puzzled before continuing, "But when I confronted him, he said I was nothing more than a step away from Bob and toward him. I was nothing to either of them. Oh, he was hilariously crowing that if I was as bad at playing Don Juan as I was at playing the jilted lover he wasn't surprised that Sunny had thrown me over. I'm afraid that was when I lost my grip. Incapacitated him with a chop to the Adam's apple then throttled him. He was surprised. But thank God for driving gloves. He might have struggled, but he left nary a scratch. That's never happened to me before. I've always been in control; I don't lose."

"You'll forgive me if my sympathy lies with the boyfriend. I think he lost much more than his temper," Vicki responded coldly. She persisted, "And what about Sunny? Are even friends the victims of your bad temper?"

For a moment, David seemed confused, but he finally continued, "I didn't mean that, either. I came back after we went to look for Tim; I was afraid Sunny might put two and two together. I wanted to talk to her. I still had that key from when the house was our trysting place, and, anyway, you hadn't locked up. You weren't in the room. So I closed the doors. Sunny was antagonistic, even suspicious. She caught on to me right away. The woman said some vicious things. She'd destroy me—and I remembered how when we broke up she'd threatened to make me look bad enough to cost me my position in the firm if I didn't stay away. I'd never forgiven her for that. Worse, she started to realize that I had killed her 'friend.' I knew she'd turn me in. I was afrai...overwrought, thinking you would hear and come back. I must have lost control when I strangled her. As you noticed, I sometimes forget my childhood training and use my left hand under extreme stress. Seeing how overwrought Tim was, it didn't take an Einstein to figure out that slipping into his pocket an incriminating portion of that last letter from Sunny would focus suspicion on him. "

"And how do you propose to get away with four murders in one night?" Vicki logically challenged David. She had to play this game just right; she couldn't let him sense the horror and despair eating at her. Maybe he was desperate enough to buy what she had to offer. David Morrow, cold and logical, didn't *quite* have the hang of understanding, let alone dealing with, his crimes of passion. Detachment had always been his powerful tool. Maybe without it he could be outwitted.

However, David didn't sound outwitted when he explained, "You will be found murdered on the grounds. It won't be difficult for me to slip away undetected. In a few days, I can always become terribly worried about my friends; tell the authorities that the last time I saw my chum Timothy, at dinner, he seemed troubled by something and wanted to see you and Sunny; and after a suitable time I can subtly help the police discover information about this place in the West and Addams offices. No one knows that I was here with you people tonight, except the dead, who won't be doing much talking."

"And Janos Husaruch will go along with all this?"

"Janos Husaruch's knife killed Tim. Husaruch ran off after we confronted him. I could make him look quite guilty, and as executor and lawyer for the now-deceased partnership of West and Addams, I can add or delete or change any incriminating evidence to establish my innocence while making Mr. Husaruch look quite guilty. Nothing definite enough for him to easily alibi, just circumstantial enough to raise some awkward questions if he tries any boat rocking. I suspect from Mr. Husaruch's admirable imitation of Jesse Owens, dashing off into the woods, that he is not the sort to look for trouble when there's no spotlight to make him look good. He was no Sir Galahad to leave you with me."

Vicki swallowed hard and cleverly let the bitterness she felt at this truth color her words: "True. So wouldn't you relish the chance to beat him in a way Sunny's lover beat you? Wouldn't you relish an ally against him? Your claims would be more convincing if you had a corroborating witness."

"Which means?"

"Four corpses are harder to explain than three—and a wife can't testify against her husband, but she can testify against her husband's enemy."

David's smile could have been Webster's illustration for "sardonic." He seemed genuinely delighted, all the time thinking as he spoke with admiration, "You can be deliciously vicious after all, Vicki. Admirably clever. And I have to admit I wasn't lying when I told you I'd made a big mistake letting you slip out of my hands."

"All the more desirable because I can help you even the score with Husaruch."

David continued smiling and agreed, "While I can help you even your score with him for abandoning you. Nicely done, Vicki. As I said, admirable. I don't think I could want you more than I do right now."

He smiled; she smiled, and then he put the gun back to her head. Vicki's jaw almost hit the ground.

"Too nicely done, Vicki. If you're that vicious, that clever, I don't think I'd ever feel safe with you knowing as much as you do. I'm afraid, as much as you tempt me, I'll have to take you out of the game—now."

"But the gun. They'll trace it to you," Vicki stammered as David cocked the hammer.

"Vicki, not every state requires you to register a gun you might buy. It also helps to file off the serial numbers as well. I don't like the government invading my privacy."

"But people will know you used the gun for practice yesterday. They'll know you have a gun."

"You never knew that I owned a gun—and who says that I use a range for practice? Just because I'm a city boy doesn't mean I can't find some isolated woods. I've hunted around here often enough with Tim."

"You're taking a big chance," Vicki argued, her anger and despair almost overcoming her. Even if there were holes in David's logic, he wasn't seeing them. His ultimately getting caught by the police wouldn't help her if she was dead.

"Good bye, Vicki. Sorry to end it all this way, really."

A hefty rock sang out of the darkness and caught David in the shoulder, staggering him so that the gun flew from his hand into the road, and as he stumbled, to save himself, he released Vicki. He was down on his knees, scrambling for the gun while Vicki instinctively made like Seabiscuit for the woods.

Janos had never left her! sang in her head. Had she heard him yell for her to run? She had a friend left in this nightmare. Tearing through the woods, her face and body lashed by branches, it took Vicki some time to realize that she was alone. Janos wasn't on the run with her. He must have gone after David to make sure he couldn't hunt them down with his gun. He might be fighting David for their lives now! Could she abandon him? He might be giving his life for her!

Breathing hard, shaking, she stopped and leaned against a tree. Vicki could hear the two fighting beyond the trees in the woods. Slowly, her mind began to clear. Slowly, she began to realize that her rescuer might, himself, need to be rescued. Not so slowly, Vicki realized that she might have found her ally only to lose him.

Yet Vicki couldn't quite move. She'd never before been the crucial factor in, literally, a life and death struggle. Her fears were confirmed by the sudden breathless silence, broken by some cutting comment that knocking a gun out of someone's hand was ineffective unless you kept the gun out of that hand.

Vicki strained anxiously forward, her heart aching for Janos. And then she hated herself for resolutely sinking back into the dank leaves and hoping she could wait out David in the darkness of the forest and her soul. She didn't want him to shoot her.

* * * * * *

Janos Husaruch found himself sitting uncomfortably in the muck of the road. Of course what made him the most uncomfortable was the gun held on him by David Morrow. It was only now that the fog was clearing and the moon had managed to meander from behind the clouds. How heartening to actually be able to see David rigidly holding the gun on him in the moonlight. But Morrow's smile was not quite triumphant. *Now that was interesting.*

"At the risk of sounding clichéd, Morrow, there's very little chance for you to get away with killing five people."

"There's no chance of me getting away with it if I allow any of you to survive," David returned, only a slight catch in the sinister sprightliness of his voice.

"You'll never be able to turn back all the suspicion," Janos insisted. "If I were you, I'd take a proverbial 'powder' now, before anyone can catch up to you. You don't have to kill anymore."

"I can't afford to take that chance. Besides, do you honestly think I intend to give up my practice, my standing, my power when I can end all threats in a matter of seconds?"

David aimed carefully.

"Not seconds. What about Vicki? She could be hitching a ride into town even while we're speaking. Even if that isn't the case, you could blunder through the woods all night and never find her. You are a fool to make it worse when you can get away."

A touch of hope caught Janos as he saw David hesitate, pondering; but that hesitation, unfortunately, didn't last. David's ego, or maybe his desperation, was more powerful.

"I'll find her. I used to hunt here. The moon's up now—and so is your time, maestro. I regret to deprive the world of your great talent, although after a few of those cracks of yours tonight I won't mind removing the personality connected to that talent. Good night, sweet prince."

"Are all these deaths worth it?" Janos pressed.

"Husaruch, even if I weren't a lawyer, I'd still know that three murders will get me the death penalty just as quickly as five. There aren't any bargain punishment rates for capital crimes."

Without any more quotes from *Hamlet*, David raised his gun and fired—but not before a rock connected with his skull. He pitched forward, out for the count.

"Janos!"

Vicki crashed out of the woods and staggered into the road, staring at the fallen form of Janos Husaruch, lying face up in the road.

His stillness seemed to make that bitter moonlight stretch to eternity. Vicki couldn't move, almost couldn't feel.

"Is it safe yet?" came Janos's voice before he cautiously sat up, his hand touching a nasty graze on his shoulder.

"I thought you were dead," Vicki managed.

"I hope you're not disappointed."

So swiftly she hardly knew how she reached him, Vicki had wrapped her arms around Janos and both of them held each other tightly. Janos couldn't care less about his arm now.

Vicki pulled away slightly and said with a quiet smile, "You came back."

"I never left, Vicki. I tracked you through the woods. I never gave up on you."

He brushed her hair from her face and touched her cheek. Vicki looked down, her smile fading as she fumbled, "What I said to David about marrying him..."

He laughed softly and, raising Vicki's face with his good arm, said, "You spin a nice tale, Vicki. I told you before that I know what's inside you."

She smiled, not quite looking at Janos, but she had to look at him when he kissed her. It was so nice to hold him close afterwards. And then Vicki's eyes flashed open, as she realized her back was exposed to David, but she hadn't retrieved his gun.

Vicki extricated herself from a startled Janos's arms and scampered to her feet to see the gun still in David's hand—but David was lying still in the road.

Dashing over to snatch up David's weapon, Vicki was further relieved to find, after a quick pulse check, that she hadn't killed with her well-aimed stone.

"How did you do it? Knock him out?" Janos called bemusedly, nodding toward the unconscious David.

Vicki's mouth crooked into a grin and she explained, "Your pitching inspired me to remember that I always could out-toss David at snowball warfare when we were young. I guess it's a talent you never outgrow, thank God."

"I imagine I'd better stay on your good side, or at least out of range," Janos wryly surmised.

They laughed a little, Vicki's glance fell on the house, now Sunny's mausoleum. Janos saw her pain and got up, crossing to her. He held her.

"It's over," he said gently. She hugged him tightly, then looked up and asked, "Your arm?"

"Just a graze. Believe me, Vicki, if there were anything seriously wrong with this arm, I'd let you know. It's my life. But let's not tell my mother; you know how mothers worry over every little thing."

"Maybe a little chicken soup would help?"

"Not too bad for a shiksa," Janos concluded.

"A shiksa with a damned fine curve ball, or should I say 'curve rock'?"

"Something tells me that I'm going to need to start practicing ducking."

"Only if you don't behave."

This time Vicki pulled him close. It was time to step out of the past.

The End

Acknowledgements

First and foremost, I need to thank Jean Grant and Janet Raye Stevens for their enormous patience in talking me through the self-publication process. They are great friends to whom I owe so much—and wonderful writers. Buy their books. Lorraine Sharma Nelson, Mary Small, and Cheryl Marceau have also given me invaluable advice and encouragement—also good writers whose books you should buy. This time out, my posse/editors consisted of Ruth Haber, De-Ping Yang, and Judy Jeon Chapman. Thanks, Judy, for setting me straight on south paws; and, Ruth, your critique was spot on, as well as hilarious. Much thanks to early readers, way back when, Kathy Healey, Sue Gagnon, and Andrea Rossi, who told me that the initial version of *Surprise!* was worth keeping. Karasel Cover Art (www.karaselcoverart.com) created the perfect cover for my novel, capturing the sinister atmosphere with aplomb. As always, I have so much appreciation for all the friends who have supported and encouraged me through the years. You know who you are. Finally, all my thanks to my husband Yang whose encouragement, editing, and tech support make all things possible.

Sharon Healy-Yang